Th

Musical Quest of Harrison Hare

Book Two

"Journey to Rhythm Creek"

Story & Song Lyrics by:
Wade Douglas Boteler

Illustrated by:
Corinne Boteler-Drew
&
Wade D. Boteler

Technical / Formatting / Graphics / Publishing:
Kristine Hashimoto

Original title: "The Story of the Hare and His Horn" - Dec. 1973

'Resurrected' edition: "The Musical Quest of Harrison Hare" - March 2006

"The Musical Quest of Harrison Hare" - Book One published - June 2016

Special Thanks:

To my amazing family who's support and encouragement over the years made this work possible.

To Kris for her expertise, support, creative input, the drawing tablet, and most importantly, her endless patience! Love you BB!

To my sister Cori for all your time, patience, and efforts illustrating the characters bringing this story to life.

To all who purchased book one and supported this project.

To anyone working on making their dreams come true and animal lovers worldwide.

"The Musical Quest of Harrison Hare"

Book Two – 'Journey To Rhythm Creek'

Book one synopsis:

Harrison Hare is an adored member of the Glade community; always willing to pitch in and help where needed.

One day, Hare was bored out of his mind when his best friend, Yungbuck, suggested trying a new activity like writing, painting, or perhaps trying a musical instrument.

That's all it took for Hare to find his father's old trumpet and start to play it, and play it, and play it some more!

While wandering around trying to find anyone to perform for, Hare happened upon a town meeting; a meeting about him.

The town's people were searching for a solution to the problem of the noise Hare was making. To him, he thought he played beautifully, but the reality was much different.

This rejection crushed him as he tucked his father's horn under his arm and bolted into the forest where many dangers unknown to him waited.

Also unknown to Hare, Owl the town's Mayor, alerted the regions magistrate, Hazel-Mae to help him since no one else could. She wanted to take him to a place where he could flourish.

Hazel-Mae's big question remained however: Would young Harrison have what it takes to venture into the dark unknown and face certain dangers to make his dreams come true?

This is the account of their journey toward that ultimate goal:

Chapter One

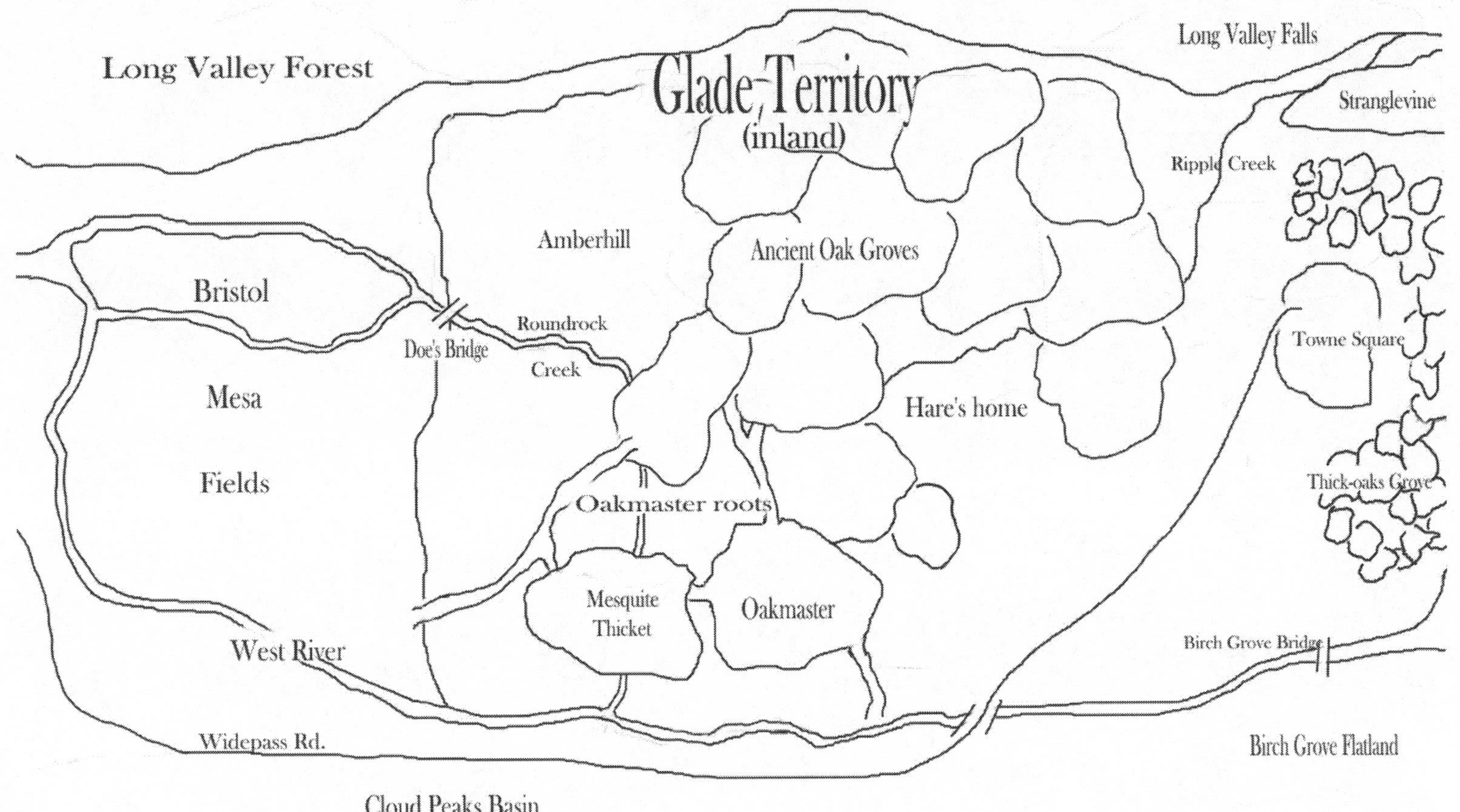
Glade Territory
(inland)
Long Valley Forest
Long Valley Falls
Stranglevine
Ripple Creek
Amberhill
Ancient Oak Groves
Bristol
Roundrock
Doe's Bridge
Creek
Mesa
Fields
Hare's home
Towne Square
Thick-oaks Grove
Oakmaster roots
Mesquite
Thicket
Oakmaster
West River
Birch Grove Bridge
Widepass Rd.
Birch Grove Flatland
Cloud Peaks Basin

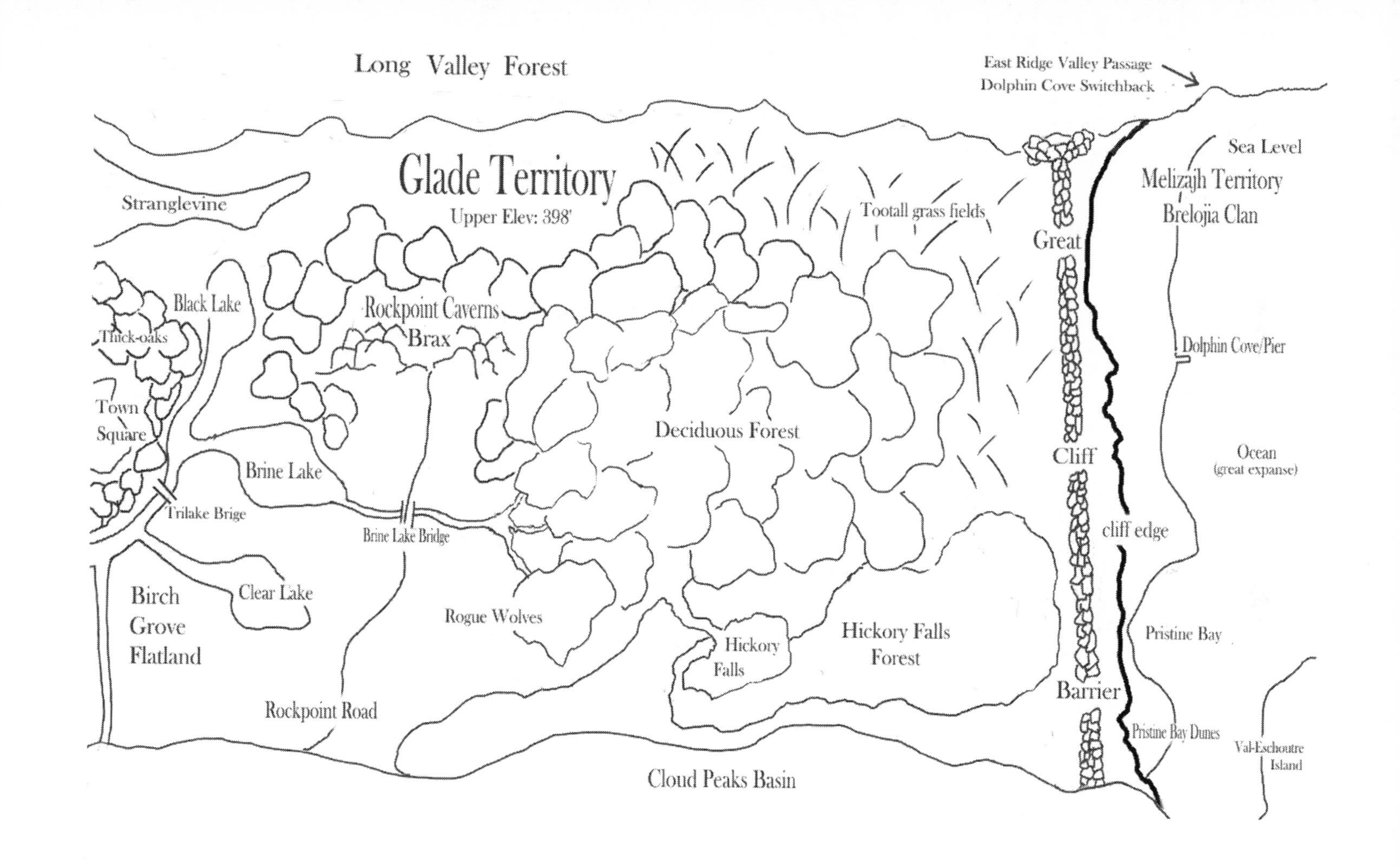
Long Valley Forest
East Ridge Valley Passage
Dolphin Cove Switchback
Glade Territory
Upper Elev: 398'
Stranglevine
Sea Level
Melizajh Territory
Brelojia Clan
Tootall grass fields
Great
Cliff
Barrier
cliff edge
Black Lake
Thick-oaks
Rockpoint Caverns
Brax
Dolphin Cove/Pier
Town
Square
Deciduous Forest
Ocean
(great expanse)
Brine Lake
Trilake Brige
Brine Lake Bridge
Birch
Grove
Flatland
Clear Lake
Rogue Wolves
Hickory Falls
Forest
Hickory
Falls
Pristine Bay
Pristine Bay Dunes
Val-Eschoutre
Island
Rockpoint Road
Cloud Peaks Basin

Harrison Hare turned and blindly ran as fast as he could away from the Town Square toward the Thick Oaks grove. He doubted anyone would come after him. Why would they when they just sent him away?

Try as they might, thought a sobbing Hare, even the sparrows and Owl wouldn't be able to find him within the labyrinths of hollowed out logs, reed thickets, and boulders which led to the river.

He stopped running and hid beneath a large mound of downed branches where he quickly made a strap for his trumpet out of reed strips; now he could run flat out on all four legs.

Deciding to rest, Hare waited and listened.

He heard faint commotion from the town square and was surprised after all. Owl and the sparrows were converging to hunt for him. Hare immediately took off heading toward the West River at Tri-lakes. Once there, no one would find him.

He was successful in remaining transparent as Owl, the sparrows, and even the dragonflies all took flight in the search. They flew directly over him but didn't see him blending in with the landscape.

Hare could see the soaring posse drift to the left toward Brine Lake. As soon as they were out of sight, like a blur he took off and was gone.

As he ran, he heard Owl screech off in the distance, "Hare, be careful, it's dangerous out there. Seek out Hazel-Mae. We will look after your house."

After crossing Trilake bridge at Clear Lake, he finally stopped running and hid under a berm within the convenient reed overgrowth.

Now he was alone. He was also wet and cold. The longer he sat there pondering the results of his actions, the more he began to shiver. His only option now was to have a conversation with himself which he did when such quandaries presented themselves...

"Good job carrot brain. You've managed to run away from the only home you've ever known.... and, you also don't have any food, blankets, or shelter not to mention the fact that you'll soon become lost since you've never gone past Rockpoint Road in your entire life."

"You can always go back and discuss it with Owl; you know, start over again; find a solution."

"No way! I don't understand it and I don't understand them. I'll find my own way."

He sniffled and wiped his bloodshot eyes while his tears dropped into the water. He could see his reflection morph as the tiny ripples grew.

"Guess you'll have to find a whole new life since you no longer have any friends. No one likes you and no one loves you. So-"

"I love you."

A beautiful reflection suddenly appeared beside his as he nearly fell into the river being startled. He stood up and stared wide-eyed at the angelic vision before him.

"You... you are..."

"Hello Harrison. I'm Hazel-Mae!"

"....but how did... Owl said that I should seek you out but you found me first so..."

"It appears then, that this is your lucky day after all. I am here to help you."

Hare was confused. "But... how did you know where to find me? And how did you know my name?"

"Dear Harrison. I know a great many things as this is my territory to observe."

"Yes, I know. I mean, you're a legend but how did you know the town would send me away?"

Hazel asked softly, "nobody sent you away. You sent yourself away did you not? Did you hear anyone ask you to leave?"

Hare thought for a moment as his ears drooped again, “no. No, I guess not.”

“So you chose to leave on your own, right?” asked Hazel-Mae smiling.

“Yeah, I suppose but no one wanted me there,” answered Hare looking at his feet.

“Do you remember last summer when that mocking bird kept you awake and how angry you were?”

Hare just stared at Hazel. “Of course I remember but how did you know that?” Hare stopped staring realizing it didn't matter. “Yes, I see your point. Now I really feel like a big poogin head.”

Hare stopped all movement as he thought while Hazel-Mae watched him. He then threw his arms up in the air looking up at Hazel, “so, what should I do?”

“Follow your heart Harry. Follow it as your father did. He also had to make the noise no one wanted to hear and look what he accomplished! I see no reason why you can't do the same. Just remember any dream worth your time to accomplish will not come easily.”

“I hear you,” said Hare, becoming more at ease. “I want to begin to seriously practice like Dad always did but I have to live somewhere; I can't be outside all the time, and anywhere I go the same thing will happen. And on top of all that, I have no idea what I'm doing or even how to start.”

“Well, I may have a solution for you. Have you ever met a chimpanzee?”

“A chimpanzee? No, never. Why?”

“Because I'm friends with a clan of chimpanzees who are very involved in the music scene. They have a blues band called the Rhythm Creek Boys and want to incorporate a brass section for a new sound. They're looking to begin with a trumpet player. Want the gig?”

Hare got excited and jumped up and down with his long ears

flapping. “Sure! Of course! But...”

Hare then got serious.

“But what?” asked Hazel.

“It's just, well it seems to me they would want someone who already knows what they're doing. You've seen what happens when I play.”

“That's what we're going to change! I have confidence in you. So, want to go meet them!”

Hare jumped up and down again. “Right now? Just like that? Really?”

“Yes sir, just like that,” smiled Hazel. “This is the perfect time of year to make the journey. We'll be there in about four days, five at the most but you will meet many new friends along the way as I have several stops to make. The best thing is you can practice while we walk!”

Hare chuckled, “actually the best thing is since I sound so bad we'll be safe from any dangers out there!”

Hazel laughed, “no Harry, in time you will play so beautifully you will tame the savage beast. So my fearless traveler, ready to begin?”

“Ready-rabbit, that's me! Let's do it!”

Hazel-Mae and Hare took off for the East Ridge Valley which was the only direction available to them. As Hazel-Mae mentioned, she had business along that route anyway so it would be a serious learning experience for him. She wanted Hare to meet the legendary Rhythm Creek Boys with confidence and nothing would do that better than venturing into the unknown.

Hare didn't have a clue what to expect and he didn't even think about it. He was too excited because deep down he sensed something was very right about this and he was ready to embrace it dangerous or not.

Their journey began strolling through the Birch Grove Flatlands, which was near the Town Square. This is roughly where Hare was standing when he heard the town's council against his playing. As he and Hazel-Mae set out, Hare suddenly stopped with a troubled expression.

"What is it?" asked Hazel.

"I feel bad about running off like that. I should go back and at least apologize. We can do this tomorrow can't we?"

"Now Harry, if you do that you'll change your mind. Besides, you don't have to apologize-"

Hazel-Mae cupped her hands around her mouth and whistled out a perfect imitation of the sparrow's song. Within seconds, a small flock of sparrows circled her as she quietly whistled an odd but ancient melody. Instantly the flock flitted away.

"There, the sparrows will tell Owl and I'm sure he and everyone else will understand. The important thing is that we need to leave right away so as to be well past Brine Lake by nightfall. That way we'll have plenty of time to rest. I have a friend there who will put us up."

Hare hesitated, thinking, then smiled, "okay, great! Sounds good to me. You know what? This is fun! Tell me about the chimpanzee people."

Hazel-Mae laughed. "chimpanzee people! You're not far off! They're people to me but you will meet many different *people* but whether they're human or not, they all have a rich history. Like our second stop, my family, the Brelojia Clan. We all appear to be human children but are actually full grown adults. We never age past what in human years would be around 12 to 15 but live regular human lifespans. But the chimpanzee people are very special friends. Just wait and see. You will have no better teachers I assure you!"

Now Hare was excited! "Like I said, sounds good to me! Maybe by the time we get to your home I'll be practiced enough to play for them before I meet your chimpanzee friends!"

Hazel-Mae stopped and held Hare's hands in hers. "My dear Harrison, you'll not only play for them, but with them! Wait until you hear our band! You'll love jamming with them and don't worry about being a beginner either. Just play and do your best because that's how you'll learn. All good things not only take effort, but patience as well. The Rhythm

Creek Boys would say the same thing."

For the first time since he ran off, Hare held his Father's trumpet with serious intentions to learn how to play it now that he had guidance. He placed his fingers just right remembering watching his father, and Hazel-Mae was expecting him to start playing but he just stared at it.

"Well, go ahead", said Hazel-Mae. "Let your fear float away like a feather in the wind. It's just us now, besides, it's either do it or don't do it. Don't forget your father had to endure the same thing. It's important to always remember the only way to instantly eliminate your fear is to act on it. Your Dad did it and you can too so c'mon, honk away maestro, let me hear what-cha got!"

Hare chuckled, "okay, but don't forget you asked for it!"

Hare started to play but after the first series of really sour notes he stopped with an equally sour look on his face. "Whoa! I don't blame everyone for complaining about me; I sound like a pond full of ducks. Time to get busy. "

Hazel-Mae laughed. "You'll get there Harry. Just remember, you must remain focused on that dream and practice even when you don't feel like it. So, I'll be quiet now because I want to hear some noise!"

"Noise? That, I can do!"

Hare continued to search for a clean note as they strolled along. No sooner did he find one, he would relax his lip pressure which would produce another sour note. Hazel-Mae giggled because she saw that he wasn't about to give up; she also saw he wasn't getting frustrated and that was a very good sign indeed!

Right when Hazel started to hear Hare improving, he stopped and rubbed his face. Hazel chuckled watching his expressions when Hare turned to her.

"What? My whole face hurts."

"Of course it does because you're not used to it. You're starting to sound better though. Maybe don't try so hard, you know? Slow it down and instead of trying to play a tune, work on holding long, sustained notes.

You'll get to scales later. Crawl before you walk, walk before you run Harry!"

"Right. Okay, I'll try that." Hare took a few steps then started playing again. This time he followed Hazel's advice and started to hold notes then added more notes without any pauses or breaks. Hazel smiled knowing he would do well on this journey. She was originally worried about whether or not he'd even want to go.

With the Brine Lake bridge coming into view off in the distance, Hare's playing starting to sound pretty good! Hazel began to dance around in circles with her long black hair gently drifting with her movements.

Suddenly Hazel-Mae's graceful dance stopped abruptly but Hare was in the moment and kept playing. Hazel made a rapid hiss sound which alerted Hare instantly.

"Don't move a muscle," whispered Hazel.

Hare didn't budge but could easily see the glaring reflection from the hungry eyes from within the dense foliage of the forest. Within minutes they were surrounded by a pack of snarling, drooling wolves.

Hazel-Mae knew all of the wolf clans and could communicate with them. As she silently feared, this pack did not follow the very organized society of a wolf pack who's honor is legendary. This pack were rogue's and when Hazel's attempts to communicate fail, she relied on her defense mechanism.

She opened her mouth as if screaming but Hare hears nothing. The wolf pack, however, goes berserk, blindly howling into the air and barking uncontrollably. They retreat back into the thick foliage and all seems well for the moment but Hazel-Mae knows the rogues are far from being scared off.

Sure enough, the pack returns snarling even more now. Hazel repeats the pitch and then repeated it even higher but the wolves aren't phased by it at all.

Hare remained motionless but for the first time he sees Hazel-Mae frightened. He realizes her attempts to drive away the menace isn't working and is now afraid, perhaps fearing for her life. After all, she is still basically a very small human and the wolves see this. A very small human and a tiny rabbit would be no match.

Hare hears Hazel-Mae's slight whimper of impending fear. This was too much for him so without thinking he reacted.

As the starving wolves began to close the snarling circle they've tightened around them, something changed in Hare upon hearing Hazel-Mae's fright.

He takes his trumpet and starts blasting out the worst notes he could manage. Luckily that wasn't a problem but he also commenced his popular nutty-bunny dance while flapping his long ears erratically from side to side, making faces.

When he see's the pack back off a bit, he starts yelling as if crazy while honking his horn and acting completely out of his mind. Meanwhile, Hazel remains still watching this but is amazed by what Hare does next.

The wolf pack did back off but are voracious eaters and are starving so they persisted but cautiously. Hare noticed their hesitation and used it to his advantage. As they crept slowly toward Hazel, Hare attacks the pack by running toward them wailing on his horn then wildly swinging it while screaming like distemper.

Only now the wolves actually see the swinging, gleaming trumpet. The pack is frightened by the sight of it since they don't know what it is or what its capable of. Hare finally lifts his trumpet and blows the highest note he can but sustains it long enough for the wolf pack to give up as they howl and run back into the forest.

Hazel-Mae doesn't move but watches as Hare stands his ground ready to take on any and all foes. He continues to yell like a mad-bunny while swinging his trumpet making sure they know he's serious.

Finally he stops, breathing heavily but doesn't move; watching all around him to protect Hazel-Mae. Feeling confident the wolves have retreated for now, he turned toward Hazel still keeping vigilant of their surroundings.

Hazel-Mae ran to Hare and surprised him with a bear hug as tears streamed down her face.

“Thank you. Thank you Harry. You saved my life. I'll never forget it!”

“You saved mine first! Wait – shhhh,” commanded Hare. “Someone's coming, sounds like a horse and cart.”

“That's my friend from Rockpoint.”

Hare looked over at her, “and is his timing always so perfect?”

Hazel smiled, “actually, he's never on time... he's always early. We better get back on the road, rogue wolves don't give up for long.”

“You don't have to tell me twice,” said Hare as he helped Hazel-Mae up the berm leading to the road to Brine Lake bridge.

Hare stood with horn in hand like a weapon watching their surroundings saying over his shoulder, laughing...

“I remember you saying one day I might play good enough to tame the savage beast. Ha, I sent the beasts running with tails tucked! Man do I need practice!”

Chapter Two

The horse and cart came to a squeaky stop as Hare continued to keep watch. He expected to see one of Hazel-Mae's animal kingdom friends or perhaps one of her kin but to Hare's amazement it was...

"Brax??? Mr. Braxton? That can't be you!!!"

"Hello Harry! Long time son!"

Billy Brax, as he used to be called, was the only human member of Hare's father's band, "The Cave Dwellers". After Hare's father passed away, then his mother left him, Billy Brax moved in with Hare to help him cope with the double trauma. To Hare, Brax was like a second father and hadn't seen him since.

Hare instantly exploded in tears as did Hazel since she expected it. The two embraced but their reunion was short lived as they made haste getting into the cart before the wolf pack returned.

They sped off as everyone was jostled from side to side over the bumpy old road. Hare sat sandwiched between Brax and Hazel and all was silent for a few seconds until Hare began to weep again. It was a combination sad and happy emotion which they all felt.

"Look at you," exclaimed Brax, "you're all grown up Harry! Your father would be very happy to see his trumpet tucked safely under your wing! And if what I heard was you playing, you're gonna need some help son!"

Between his sniffling and broken voice, Hare managed to laugh.

"Yes, as much as I can get! Wow, Mr. Braxton, you were Dad's very best friend and mine too. It is so good to see you!"

"Great to see you too Harry. I've been retired for a long time. In fact, the last full-on jam I had with your father was the last gig I played. After your Dad passed, I kind of lost interest in it. I lost interest in everything."

"Yeah, me too." Replied Hare. "You went somewhere didn't you? I haven't seen you since."

“I decided to just take off and experience new things; you know, trying to clear the brain with new sites and sounds. I finally settled here at Rock Point. It's a perfect location for me.”

The three sat in silence for most of the ride. There were so many different emotions but the best thing was about to occur which Hazel was looking forward to.

Brax continued-

“...and since I've been at Rock Point, I've had time to reflect on the old days and settled into some form of a comfortable life. So when Hazel-Mae came to me asking if I could accommodate you before your journey begins I was happy to help. Besides, I have some surprises for you.”

Like everyone, Hare loved surprises but instead of getting all excited he was serious and looked up at Hazel-Mae.

“So, this trip was planned?”

“Yes,” answered Hazel-Mae. “Many things were planned except for you running off like you did. I'm lucky to have found you.”

“You're right there.” admitted Hare,” I shouldn't have done that. Pretty childish of me but I don't understand how this could be all planned out so quickly-”

“Here we are,” said Brax as he stopped the cart. He stepped down and rolled the wooden door open, climbed back on then slowly drove everyone inside his dwelling. “Careful of the terrain, it can be slippery. It flattens out once you're in the gallery.”

Hazel smiled and said to Hare, “We'll fill you in on everything Harry.” Hazel then turned to Brax, “want me to stable Miss. Bliss?”

“Yes, please if you would. And I will light a fire and get some food cooking.” Brax then rolled the gate-door closed sealing them safely inside.

Hazel looked around nodding her head, “impressive! You've done a lot of work to this place since I was here last!”

"Thank you," replied Brax, "always trying to improve the man-cave!"

"I'll be right back." said Hazel as she led Miss Bliss and the cart down the right-hand corridor toward the stable area.

Hare looked around and was amazed at how comfortable Brax's place was. He understood though since Brax helped his father bore out the huge petrified oak root to form his home.

"Nice job Mr. Braxton!"

"Harry would you please call me Brax. I'm trying to simplify things in my advanced years."

Hare chuckled, "sorry Brax. Nice work on the stairway."

"Thanks. Guess who taught me that?"

"Yeah, Pop taught me a lot also but he left too soon."

Brax lit the potbelly stove while opening the flue then turned to Hare.

"Yes he did. He had so much insight, man. He taught me about composition and, of course," Brax motioned around the cave ceiling and staircase, "building all of this too so when he passed on, I was messed up like you were. Things back then were unstable as you know....and...your Pop and me were younger and hadn't yet been introduced to wisdom. Be that as it may, there sure were a lot of great times, which reminds me-"

Brax walked into another room as Hare wandered around looking at Brax's home. He almost got emotional because he recognized his fathers work in many places.

After a few moments Brax walked back into the room carrying a large trunk. He sat the trunk down next to his chair taking a seat across the table from Hare.

"Hand me that horn you got there." Brax took the old beat up trumpet and fiddled with the valves and then held it to his lips and played some really sour notes.

"Wow Harry! Did you have this bell under water or something? Look at this! Poor thing is worn out man. See? Look at these valves here. The pads are nearly gone. Try this one instead."

Brax carefully pulled out a small case and handed it to Hare.

"This was your Dad's prized possession. This trumpet is a B flat with mute and case. It may as well be brand new since your Pop babied this thing man! Go ahead son, check it out. It's yours now!"

Hare reached out and gently took the case as if it were a newborn baby. His watering eyes were trying to stay open as he was obviously overwhelmed.

Just then Hazel appeared from the stable corridor, "Go ahead. Open it!"

Hare unlatched the locks and slowly opened the lid. There was a clean cloth covering it which Hare removed. He gasped upon seeing the gleaming instrument. He could clearly see his reflection in the bell!

Both Brax and Hazel expected him to get emotional but he surprised them. He lifted the trumpet out of the case and held it up gazing at it. Instead of crying with joy he just stared and said...

"Blazin' bell man!"

Brax started clapping and laughed out loud since that was a popular saying in his day and was surprised Hare knew it. Hazel was clapping too since she knew that Brax wasn't done with the gifts yet.

"Here, I'll take that gorgeous bell, you take this."

Reaching back into the chest, Brax pulled out a leather bound satchel and handed it to Hare.

"Here are many of your Father's compositions, lyrics, and notes to himself. What you hold in your hands is all you need to discover your own unique style. Once you find that groove, just keep working to improve it. Everything else will fall into place."

Hare was amazed. He took the heavy satchel and pulled out a few pages. He began to read the first page: "…mouthpiece placement, wet lips vs dry matter of choice, posture is important as it assists breathing, valves always push straight down, practice as much as you rest, embo... embosh..."

"Embouchure," corrected Brax. " Basically its a fancy word for lip pressure and how your facial muscles need to be used. It's different for everyone but we'll talk about that later. What you have there son are the basics. We all have to start somewhere which is usually at the beginning so I figure by the time you reach Rhythm Creek, you'll at least be practiced enough to follow those nutty chimp critters!"

Hare sat up excited. "You know the chimpanzee people!?!"

Brax laughed, "chimpanzee people! They'd love that. You're not far off!"

"Hazel said the same thing," exclaimed Hare. "Tell me about them!"

"Sure, yeah, I know the Rhythm Creek boys. Zilla was a nut man, probably still is! Well, so is Mombo but he's a bit more reserved. His brother Bombo is the opposite while Little Kong is the youngest and Wombat is the smartest and they all have fleas! Yeah man," said Brax through laughter, "it's been quite a while; long time indeed. Last time we worked together was with the Kat Klan Brass. What a gig that was! We played to a packed field and the very last number turned into a serious train wreck but man, he had fun!"

Hare stood up so fast he nearly dropped the satchel. "Hey, why don't you come with us!!!" The excited Hare tuned to Hazel-Mae. "He can go right?"

"Like I said, he'll be gone for quite a while in a few days," reminded Hazel.

"Oh yeah," said Hare, sitting back down disappointed, "I forgot."

"Yep, got lots of business to tend to and many miles to go," said Brax. "But Hazel-Mae knows how to contact me so when you get back home, give me a few days and I'll be there. Besides, the Glade territory ain't that far if you know all the right short-cuts."

"You guys really did plan this out didn't you?" asked Hare. "I don't know what to say; that so many would do so much for me. How do I thank you?"

"Truth is Harry, you don't," replied Brax. "Like your home, this has all been willed to you. You have just inherited your father's favorite and famous bell, his personal notes and manuscripts, the works! But whether you inherited his amazing talent, well, that remains up to you. That son, is something no one can give you but you. Always remember Harry, no one can make your dreams come true but the one staring back at you in the mirror."

Hazel-Mae looked over at Hare and smiled. "He's right Harry. You'll do great! Just take your time and don't rush it."

Hare just sat looking down at the papers showing his dad's hand writing and almost had another emotional issue but instead was thinking. He looked down at the horn he found in the floor-box at home and the new one...

"Why would Pop have two trumpets though, aren't they the same key?"

Brax smiled and gave Hazel a quick glance indicating that Hare was indeed a thinker. This pleased him because it meant Hare was serious.

"Yeah but that old thing you've been slingin' over your shoulder was his kick-around bell. Not that he literally kicked it around but when you're hangin' in a new town, anything can happen so you have a kick-around bell in case you find yourself in an improvised jam. Those can happen anytime but you always save your best bell for the payin' gig."

"Understood," said Hare as he lifted the new trumpet up to his lips then turned to Brax.

"Would you care to jam sir?"

JAZZ

Chapter Three

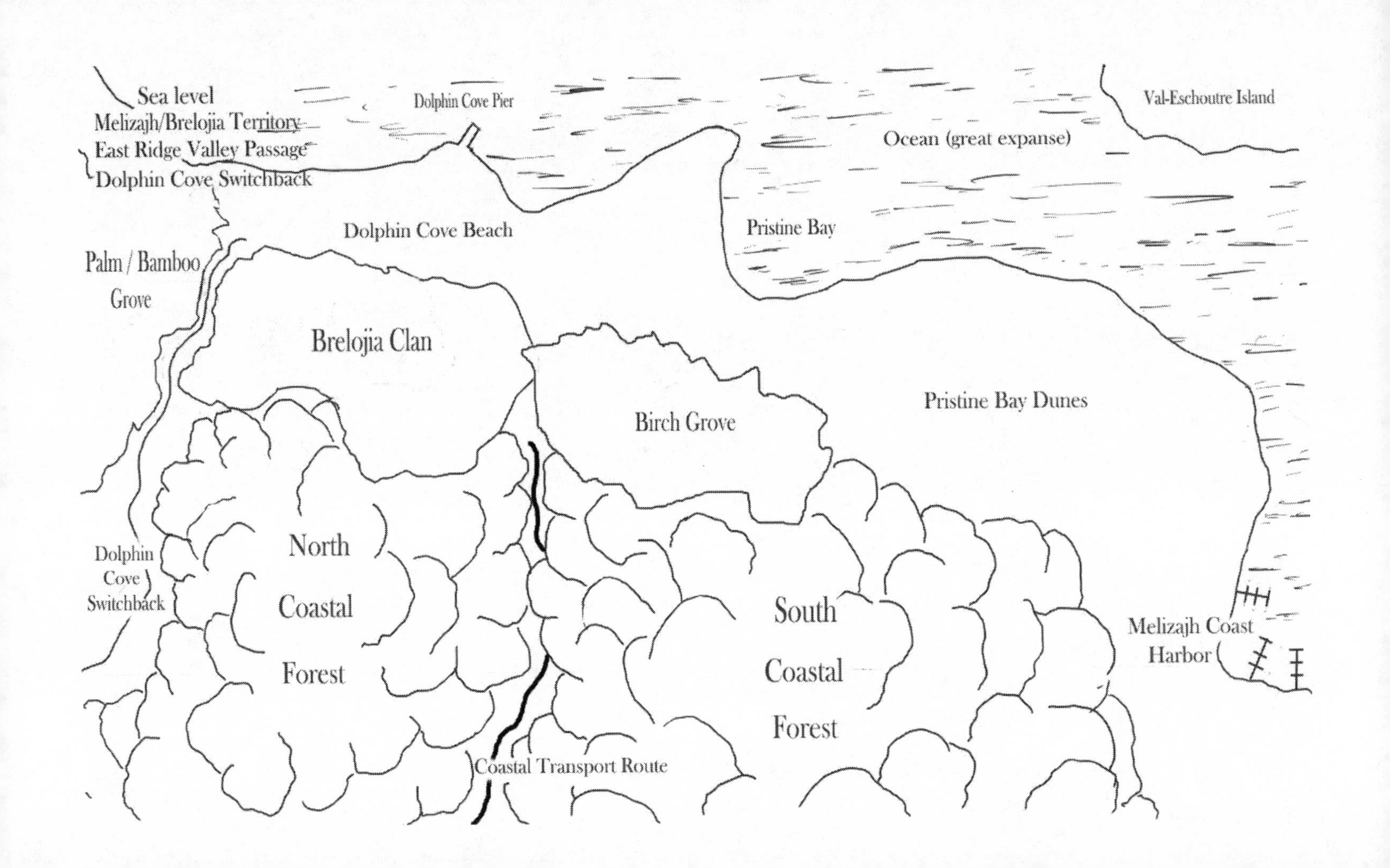
Sea level
Melizajh/Brelojia Territory
East Ridge Valley Passage
Dolphin Cove Switchback
Dolphin Cove Pier
Ocean (great expanse)
Val-Eschoutre Island
Dolphin Cove Beach
Pristine Bay
Palm / Bamboo
Grove
Brelojia Clan
Birch Grove
Pristine Bay Dunes
Dolphin
Cove
Switchback
North
Coastal
Forest
South
Coastal
Forest
Melizajh Coast
Harbor
Coastal Transport Route

Hare and Brax stayed up until Hare fell asleep with his new horn in hand. Brax tried to mentor him as long as he could since his time was limited but decided to put them up one more day to give them additional time to rest. This would also give Brax one more day to teach the basics so Hare could continue his journey with some fundamentals to practice.

The morning came quickly and it was such a beautiful day Hare was eager to hit the road. Hazel-Mae had prepared a delicious Brelojian breakfast for everyone and remained extremely grateful for Brax's hospitality. She too was tired from her grueling schedule and welcomed the prolonged rest. Plus, for Hazel-Mae to see Hare grow as a budding musician right before her eyes made her smile.

Their next stop to Brelojia would be a perfect stop for Hare to get up on stage for the first time and play with their particular style of musicians. Hazel was certain Hare didn't have a problem with what is universally known as, 'stage fright', but if so, he'd lose that fear by the time they reached Rhythm Creek.

Brax was helping Hare with his scales when he stood up and instructed him to continue practicing until he returned from an errand. He was gone for about an hour and returned with a few friends.

Hare and Hazel got up and walked outside to see several ponies complete with saddles and saddlebags small enough for them. Hare jumped up and immediately did his bunny-dance thing while Hazel-Mae was truly surprised. For someone who seemed to know everything, she sure didn't see this coming.

“William Harold Braxton, where did you get these adorable ponies?”

“I traded three cords of hickory for this brother and sister team. Since I only have room for Miss. Bliss and the cart, a friend who lives close keeps them for me. Can't have an angel and a prodigy walking all the way to rhythm creek! That would be one long trek!”

“So who's who?” asked Hare petting one of them. “ What are their names?”

“The one who's enjoying your attention is Belle. That guy over there is her brother, Blaze.”

Hare laughed, "Blaze n' Belle! Clever! Thank you Brax," said Hare, while Hazel-Mae nodded in agreement, "I wasn't expecting ponies; actually I wasn't expecting anything. I remain in your debt sir."

"There is no debt to pay but there will be if you don't keep working on those scales during your trip!"

They filled their saddle-bags and tied provisions to the saddles. Hazel and Hare were now finally ready to set off on the next leg of their journey in comfort.

"Okay, you are ready rock and roll." Brax petted both of his ponies lovingly. "Take care of my babies. I'll pick them up when I see you back at the Glade. Be safe and you," said Brax pointing to Hare, "keep practicing. I expect to hear amazing things when I see you again. And Harry, tell Barney from me that he's such a pretty boy!"

"Who's Barney?" asked a curious Hare.

"You will know in time," said Brax giving Hazel a quick glance..

"Hey Brax," asked Hare thinking, "what if I'm with the chimpanzee's for a long time? What if I'm there for years? Won't Blaze and Belle think somethings wrong?"

"No, they won't care. In fact, you'll be doing us all a huge favor. My neighbor usually boards them for me but is gone for about a year so I can't keep them there. And, I have tons of neglected business to deal with so they're all yours until I see you back at the Glade. I know I can trust their well being to your care."

"Of course you can. How cool!" exclaimed Hare then whispering into Belle's ear, "we don't have a problem with that do we Belle?"

After a fond farewell, Hazel and Hare rode away out of sight rounding the bend which led through the southern most edge of Long Valley Forest. From there the East Ridge Valley passage would connect them to the long but gently descending path known as the Dolphin Cove Switchback. That would lead them to the east beaches of the Great Expanse, or as most call it, the ocean.

First though, they had to ride down the switchback which would take them from around 400' elevation down to sea-level. Even though the switchback was a gradual downward grade, it still had to be traveled carefully.

The ride through the Long Valley Forest was a beautiful experience. As Hazel told Hare, this time of year was a perfect time to make the trip. It was springtime and another glorious summer was right around the corner.

What Hare loved most about it was the boundless life all around them; flower fields in full bloom, the many species of birds all singing their own special songs, clouds of baby insects learning to fly, newborn animals following Mom learning how to hunt, and fresh, bright green wild-grass for a carpet to ride over. For Hare, it was like waking up for the very first time!

This inspired him so he very carefully pulled out his new trumpet and began to play. He didn't practice scales, he just played. He found what he thought was a nice melody and repeated it several times.

Once again, just like their jam before being interrupted by the wolves, Hazel-Mae began to hum to it at first then started singing with her angelic voice. He just kept playing and noticed the two ponies liked it also as they altered their walk into a prance! Hare couldn't help but wonder what it would sound like with Hazel-Mae's Brelojia band. He was beyond happy!

After a while Hare stopped playing.

"Why did you stop," asked Hazel stopping her pony?

Hare lowered his trumpet and looked over at her. "I've never felt like this. I've never had experiences like this. All this wonderful brand new life everywhere makes me think of home."

Hazel looked over at him, "Harry, it hasn't even been two days! But I can understand you missing your home already."

"Well yeah, of course I do but I've had plenty of time to think about it; I was just a big baby running off like that. I only thought of myself. I'm actually embarrassed for being such a big fat whining bunny-butt."

Hazel had to laugh. "Bunny-butt? You crack me up Harry but think about this. It hasn't even been two days and look at you now! Yes, granted you were immature and really didn't think before you acted but that's normal. Usually, it takes certain youth years to grow up and pass over that threshold into maturity. I'd say you nailed it in less than two days! I've said it before, you are a thinker. The simple, but all important lesson here is that we all learn by doing. So, keep playing or I'll tell Brax!"

Hazel didn't show it but she was beaming inside! As they rode down the switchback, it seemed that with every bend they took, she heard Hare getting better and better! She wanted to compliment him but decided to just relax, listen, and enjoy one of her favorite places.

The Dolphin Cove switchback was a popular and beautiful pathway from the higher elevation of the Long Valley forest to the beaches of Brelojia and Pristine Bay Dunes. The Melizajh Territory offered a mesmerizing blend of bamboo, palm groves, birch orchards, and sprawling patches of oaks that served as astonishing welcome scenery to Brelojia.

Suddenly Hare stopped playing, shaking his head and rubbing his cheeks.

"My face is melting again."

"You won't get over that hurdle anytime soon so take a break. Remember your father's notes, practice as much as you rest."

"Sounds good to me," said Hare

He placed his bell of choice back in its case and gently draped the polishing cloth over it.

Having placed it carefully back into his saddlebag, he took a deep breath and looked around him.

"You know... granted I've never been too far away from home, which is beautiful and I love it but this? It's breathtaking!"

"Oh yes," said Hazel, "that's one awesome though unusual thing about this entire central region; the strange mixture of trees that wouldn't normally be growing together. Wait until you see the Low Valley Timbers. You will not believe your eyes."

"Where's that?"

"That is our destination. It used to be called Cedar Forest but since the chimpanzee band made it their home, it's been called Rhythm Creek ever since. What you see around you now is certainly wonderful but the Low Timbers area is quite spectacular."

"I can't wait.... wait!" Hare pointed up into the sky. "That's a seagull!"

Hare slowed Belle and stood up in the saddle smelling the air. He jumped out of the saddle and did a serious bunny dance-

"We're at the ocean! We're at the ocean! Why didn't you tell me!?"

"Surprise! I know your father always wanted to take you there but it never happened so here you go Harry! Welcome to the beaches of Brelojia."

While Hare was doing his funny-bunny jig, he felt something hit him on the ear. He stopped and looked around then passed it off. He didn't care since he was so happy. He jumped back into the saddle and exclaimed, "lets get going! The beach can't be too far!"

He started to ride off when Hare was hit by another object. Then another. And yet another. Hazel-Mae was laughing under her breath.

"Don't worry Harry, it's the Brelojian's welcoming us. They can be quite the practical jokers."

"That's a relief. You sure I'm not covered in gull poop?"

Hazel-Mae looked him over and assured him, "no, you're poop free! The Brelojian children are tossing welcome pebbles at you. It's a tradition."

"That's cool with me!"

Hazel-Mae sang out a string of beautiful notes. It was a very short melody but it resonated throughout the many different tree groves clumped together. Hare then heard a group of singing children joining Hazel which sounded amazing since it was majestic and heart-moving like a well practiced choir.

Wasting no time, Hare quickly took out his kick-around and didn't take long before he found the key they were in and began to play along. Hazel was astonished that Hare simply fell into it like that. She laughed out loud knowing this would end up being a visit to remember!

They finally arrived on the fine, silty, sand of Dolphin Cove Beach. This made it difficult for the ponies so Hazel and Hare dismounted and walked the pair while they rounded the bend leading into Brelojia.

Hare was amazed when he saw the large group of what looked like human children approaching them with banners and singing perfectly. Off in the distance the sparkling ocean gleamed in the background resembling zillions of diamonds marching toward the opposite side of the world. Hare held his trumpet high in the air and yelled into the clear, blue sky-

“Look Pops, I'm here!”

The congregation of celebrating Brelojian's led our intrepid travelers around the palm/bamboo grove and into a covered area with a feast for all! The surrounding high swaying palms and bamboo seemed to reach the sky. Some bamboo grew so round Hare could easily crawl through the trunks if he tried.

The astonishing feast was set on a long natural flat stone table covered with a dazzling tablecloth that seemed to sparkle as if it were alive. There were vegetables of every kind and various varieties of lettuce which was one of Hare's favorites. There were large banana leaf-bowls of different flavors of dipping sauces and beautifully prepared bite sized canapes and lots of different juices. He loved apples, however apples didn't grow anywhere close but he was about to discover a new favorite – mango's!

Hare was overwhelmed and didn't know where to start especially when he saw the seafood section! He realized he had never tried it before – ever!

There were many different varieties of fish prepared in many different ways. There was Alghott, similar to Cod. Steppers, a form of Lobster but sweeter and bigger. Jumps, the particular genus of shrimp in these waters, Snakenib which is an eel but tastes like Scallops, and the delicious Brelojian version of bouillabaisse aptly called, Brelojio. To adorn the table and surroundings were bouquets of the most beautiful flowers Hare had ever seen and the natural aroma was incredible!

Finally after Hare's amazement turned into a rumbling stomach, the congregation sat joking, laughing, and feasting! Hazel-Mae could see that Hare was not afraid to try new things as he would taste a little of this, a little of that, then stand up to see what was over there, 'gotta try that too'! But it was the Brelojio that sent him over the top! Everyone was surprised seeing what an appetite a small bunny had!

After a great time eating some of the best brand new food he had ever tried, Hare broke away from the festivities and headed straight for the breakwater. For him to finally go walking in the surf for the first time was literally a dream come true!

That's when it happened.

The stand-up bass started first with a simple but melodic bass line. Then the drums came in followed by bamboo marimba's Hare heard for the first time, then even more Island percussion! Meanwhile the band still kept the same beat but built in volume when the guitar came in playing an offbeat rhythm that stopped him in his tracks! The band then just cut loose filling the early afternoon with a simple but very pleasing style of music Hare had never heard before. He would learn later this particular style of music was called Reggae.

All he needed to hear was this new style to make him do an abrupt 'about-face' and run toward the band. Hazel-Mae was watching from the stage area and rarely saw him run on all fours but was surprised how fast he was when he wanted to be.

It didn't take long for Hare to reach the stage but he didn't go straight for his trumpet as Hazel-Mae expected. Instead, he just stood at the edge of the stage staring at the drummer tapping his long foot which kept perfect time. Hazel-Mae scratched her head wondering what he was doing!

The rhythm was an easy common-time beat that Hare knew his

father called four/four, but what was that other amazing sound? To Hare it sounded metallic; like the sound Beaver Boz made back home hammering away fixing Doe's Bridge. But the metallic sound were notes! What in the world was that thing?!?

To Hare, this odd instrument looked like an inverted tortoise shell that the player struck with mallets but only in certain areas. This new sound was amazing to Hare. Finally, Hazel walked over and said into his ear, “they're called steel-drums. Go pick a bell and bunny hop up on that stage!”

Hare clapped his hands together and wasted no time grabbing the new bell. He fiddled and fudged a bit but found the key as he stepped onto the stage.

The song was a slow but lively 'feel-good' tune making it fairly easy to play. Although a trumpet wasn't the type of instrument you'd find in this style of music, Hare didn't know that; wouldn't have mattered anyway!

Hare felt good about the tune and where he had to be. He didn't bury the band but knew when to come in, when to fill, when to be quiet, and when to solo! But then he was still a beginner and showed it on the last note of the tune. The vocalist held the last note perfectly as did Hare until he allowed his lip pressure to waver just enough to hit the most sour note imaginable.

The band nearly fell off the stage laughing and the audience thought it was planned but Hazel knew Hare made a mistake! Luckily, it was a huge hit! At first Hare's face turned red in embarrassment until he thought about it then started cracking up himself! He addressed the audience through broken laughter.

“... and that's what the key of H flat sounds like!”

“Wait!” Hazel walked up onto the stage to make a necessary announcement. “With all the excitement and your wonderful greeting, I have neglected proper introductions. I do apologize! My Brelojian family, please meet Mr. Harrison Hare of the Glade Territory! He is-”

She was interrupted by tremendous applause because everyone liked Hare and wanted to hear and see what would happen next! Hazel waited for the applause to diminish then continued.

"-Mr. Hare is a fledgling musician on what has begun to be a fantastic journey all the way to the Cedar Forest and the Low Valley Timbers. Harry," Hazel-Mae waved her hand over the crowd," these are the Brelojians! And here is the band you're playing with; this is Duggle on drums and percussion. Lanim, lead guitar. Jaimz rhythm guitar. Reen on bass, Jakesun on Sax, and Betzo has the best voice this side of Long Valley Forest!"

"Friends and family," announced Betzo, "please welcome Mr. Harrison and our sister Hazel-Mae to our home. Now it's my pleasure, and soon to be yours, to ask our sister Hazel-Mae to join in song and help us all sing our anthem!"

The applause of all those in attendance was almost deafening!

The band began a very upbeat, but also offbeat reggae tune that made Hare anxious to join in! When Betzo began to sing it sounded angelic. When Hazel-Mae joined her, the harmony was heavenly! Hare shook his head in disbelief since their voices were unlike anything he had ever heard but the band was funky and fun! When Hare found the groove and began playing very quietly at first, then cut loose, it was simply amazing!

We laugh, we dance, we play, we sing,

We love everyone and everything,

The ocean is our front yard, the forest is our back,

Music is our language and that's a fact!

Always peaceful is the way we be,

Always happy for new company,

Always ready to have some fun,

Always playing in the sun.

If we don't know you, that's okay,

Feel free to join our feast anyway,

Tap your feet or dance to our song,

We'll teach you the words so you can sing along

So be peaceful and happy with us today,

We'll take your troubles far, far away,

Just chill with us and you will see,

Being laid-back and cool is our decree,

Always peaceful is the way we be,

Always happy for new company,

Always ready to have some fun,

Always playing in the sun.

After more great live music and revelry, everyone gathered at the feasting table for a break and snacks. It was an amazing moment for Hare to hear all of the stories told by the Brelojian's. He was surprised to learn the Brelojian's are skilled metal-smiths which explained the drum set cymbals. Since ocean air is damaging to most metals, the Brelojian craftsmen and women, utilize deep caverns to produce their only exported product which are parts for the many ships that travel the great expanse.

Of course living at the waters edge they are very adept at fishing and trapping shellfish which they trade with other local vendors.

In the days that followed, Hare became very popular especially with the children. It took him a while to see the difference since everyone looked like children but he figured it out and knew who everyone was. This made it easy to know who to pull practical jokes on and who not to!

Because Hare had never been to the ocean before, he had never heard of body-surfing. No sooner did he see several swimmers slicing across the waves, he couldn't wait to try it probably because he was sure he could do it.

With a little instruction and some painful wipe-out's, Hare became pretty good at it. He discovered by accident that his long, strong ears were very effective as rudders and he began doing amazing quick turns and serpentine's. He also discovered that his long feet worked great for water brakes which allowed him to do even more really cool moves, like accidental water-skiing! This led to his long feet worked great for skim-boarding in the breakwater without a board. This then led to the Brelojian's making boards for it and then adopting it as a new sport.

Yes, Hare was going to leave a very lasting impression with them - especially when he was late for the afternoon jam and the band had to wait for him to finish his swimming with the dolphins!

The band didn't mind as life in Brelojia is always slow but steady and always peaceful, especially for their new family member Hare. In fact, they named him 'Laparda-zha-Sycha', which means in Brelojian, “Crazy-fun-rabbit!” Hare was thrilled to have a name in another language!

After an unforgettable Island breakfast, Hazel and Hare said their tear-streaming goodbyes and headed toward the Dolphin Cove pier. This would mark their right turn onto the Coastal Transport Route that would lead them toward yet another grand adventure.

The morning was crisp and perfect! With the delicious ocean breeze, constant sound of crashing waves and gull-song, everyone including the ponies were in second Heaven!

Hare was daydreaming as he allowed Belle to wander too close toward the soft beach sand-

“Harry, stay close to the rim please.”

“Oh right. Sorry, I was just thinking how much I'm lovin' this beach life! I was thinking that one day I might build a little hut right over there-”

Suddenly they heard a sound behind them and turned to see Betzo approaching. Curiously, they stopped the ponies. Hazel-Mae noticed her serious expression. Betzo slowed her pony but she wasn't bringing forgotten provisions.

Chapter Four

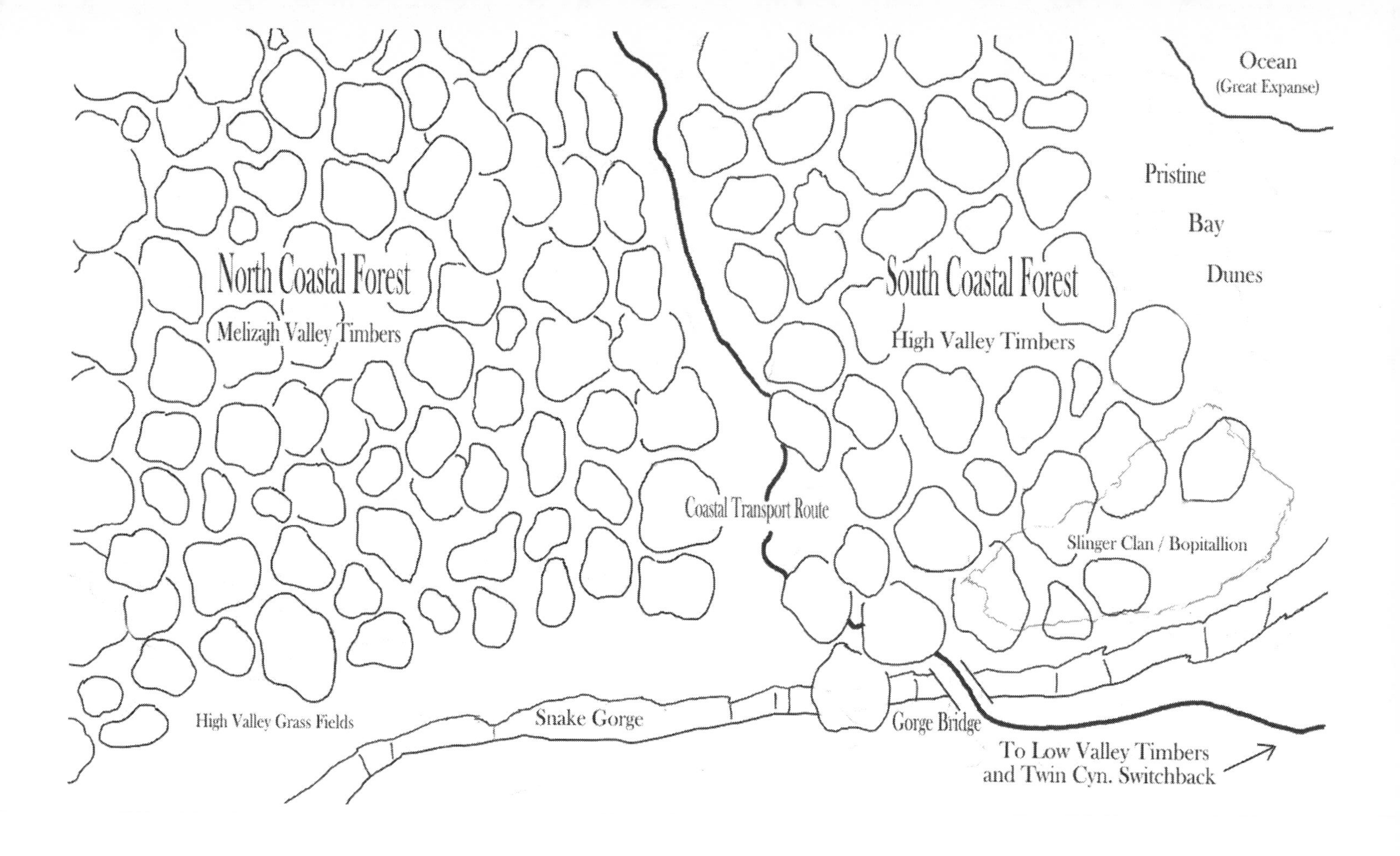
Ocean
(Great Expanse)
Pristine
Bay
Dunes
North Coastal Forest
Melizajh Valley Timbers
South Coastal Forest
High Valley Timbers
Coastal Transport Route
Slinger Clan / Bopitallion
High Valley Grass Fields
Snake Gorge
Gorge Bridge
To Low Valley Timbers
and Twin Cyn. Switchback

"Poia, Chizra, poia. Raladwai Hazil, guashai ra britasra pala-" … Betzo realized she was speaking Brelojian. "Sorry, Sister Hazel. Word just arrived that your crossing over snake gorge has been damaged. Apparently, several large oaks fell from the south forest onto the bridge. I'm sure you're aware but I had to be sure."

Hare remained quiet but was now bursting with curiosity. "What's going on? Everything cool?"

"Sister Hazel, you explain better," said Betzo.

"Well Harry, the road we planned to take normally would provide a safe crossing over Snake Gorge. Since that's gone the only other way to cross would be the old Snake Gorge Bridge." Hazel chuckled. "no one really knows how old that bridge is but it has never failed. The only problem is-"

"-well, there we go," interrupted Hare decisively.

"The only problem is," continued Hazel, "this particular bridge is too far for the ponies to walk on this sand and is many miles out of our way." Hazel turned to Betzo. "Thank you Sister, I always feared that would happen one day. We will figure out a way."

Hare was still curious. "This Snake Gorge, is it deep? Can we go around?"

Hazel once again chuckled then got serious. "Snake Gorge is roughly 67 miles long and the last time I crossed it was about 35 feet across-"

Hare interrupted again, "- that doesn't sound too bad. We could-"

"... and 312 feet straight down."

Hare didn't say a thing but then he didn't have to.

Betzo and Hazel-Mae smiled in a way that told Hare they had things under control. They all knew this region and he should just smile along with them and proceed with mouth shut which is precisely what he did.

"Forva tranqua," said Betzo as she and Hazel embraced.

"Forva tranqua bejo maga du sibli Betzhot," replied Hazel-Mae.

Betzo turned to Hare, "please keep my sister safe Mr. Harry."

"With my last breath Miss. Betzo. Thanks for the awesome jam. Don't forget about the invitation!"

"I will remember! Thank you, safata xeurfihn!"

Betzo turned her pony Chizra and rode off. There was silence between Hazel and Hare until his obvious question was asked-

"What does...safazurfin mean?"

"It means safe travels."

Hare thought for a moment and got an excited look on his face. "So, will there be danger!?!"

Hazel giggled and looked at him hearing his rising vocal inflection. "Do you want there to be danger?"

"Well," thought Hare, "not really bad danger but you know, uhmm-"

"Oh, so you're looking for nice danger." Hazel was trying to suppress her laughter now making fun of the corner Hare just talked himself into!

"No, you want comfortable danger," Hazel said jokingly, "or fuzzy-cute danger!"

Now Hare was laughing, "no, I want really happy, laughing danger! Okay I know that came out wrong but I meant that if our only road has been destroyed and we're dealing with a three hundred foot drop, I'd say there's an element of danger there."

"And you'd be right. However, we won't know for sure until we get there and assess the damage but yes, there most likely will be considerable danger. We should expect it."

They rode off as Hare settled back in his saddle having gotten used to riding. He liked it. In fact, he liked this whole adventure thing they were experiencing. Perhaps it was that now, every day he and Hazel-Mae were doing things that were new and you could never guess what would occur next even with the wildest imagination. He almost laughed out loud thinking this whole thing happened because he was bored!

They rode peacefully along and turned onto the coastal transport route. There was lush foliage, ferns, birch trees, clusters of oaks intermixed with swaying palms and high bamboo all around them. However, further ahead it appeared like a black wall where everything just stopped. Hare had been practicing some Reggae licks but seeing this abruptly stopped him. Not only did he stop playing he stopped moving.

"Wow, check it out! What going on there? Looks awfully dark."

"It's the front door to our next stop. That Harry, is the entrance to the South Coastal Forest. We're on the corridor separating the two. We stay on this road and it'll take us right to the damaged site." Hazel took a deep breath and stretched her arms. "I love this area though. Sure it's one of the denser and darker forests in my territory but in my opinion, it's the safest."

Hare looked at her curiously, "what makes a safe forest?"

Hazel looked at Hare and giggled "Oh the lack of predatory animals like that pack of rouge wolves for one thing! In fact you won't find many big, bad beasties in this dark place."

"So then, big bad beasties don't like this forest because it's dark?"

"No because the clan that lives where we're going can eat them."

Hare remained silent with a blank stare on his face until he started chuckling, "so... if they eat big bad beasties for breakfast wouldn't that make us hors d' oeuvres?"

Hazel laughed, "no silly, they're our friends! We're entering slinger country."

"......and a slinger is a...?"

"Do you have any problems with snakes?"

“Snakes? No, I like snakes. I actually have a few in my garden that eat bugs.”

“Okay, that's cool but these snakes are a bit larger. Usually twelve to twenty-five feet long and can actually split boulders if they wrap themselves around them and squeeze.”

“....that's comforting.”

“It's actually very comforting because these snakes are not only my friends but are very effective allies as they have no natural enemies.”

“Yes, no natural enemies because they ate them all! Why are they called slingers?”

“They have lived here for so long they've had to adapt to this rugged terrain. They can actually sling themselves into the gorge by freezing their bodies into a straight line and free fall until there's a tree branch they can connect to. They do that all the way to the bottom. Coming back up is easy for them so that's how they get around. It's pretty amazing. Sometimes they even have competitions to see who can sling the deepest in one fall – that is without missing and killing themselves.”

“That is pretty amazing alright but I don't think I'd want to be a judge during that contest.”

Hazel smiled as they rode toward the dense dark forest that is very safe to meet giant snakes that eat horrible beasts that can crush boulders and intentionally throw themselves into bottomless pits. Hare laughed again as he certainly wasn't bored now!

As they approached the outer fringes of the South Coastal Forest there had been no conversation just Hare practicing ad lib. Hazel loved when he just played whatever occurred to him; no rules, no thought, just play!

Hazel was smiling, listening as Hare improved. She then looked up into the sky while tilting her head to listen to something else. As soon as she began to laugh, Hare not only heard the sound of air moving, he felt it all around them.

Before Hare knew what was going on, a massive flock of large white birds with yellow rimmed feathers circled then landed on pretty much anything they wanted to. The leader of the flock perched on Hazel-Mae's shoulder. Hare had three perched on him; one on each shoulder picking at his ears and one right between them on his head. The rest of the several hundred birds seemed to be everywhere.

Hare remained still because most were displaying their 52" wingspan and had tall plumes of feathers that appeared like a crown rising above their heads indicating trouble. Hare didn't know what to do but was getting agitated.

Before Hare could respond, the leader let out a quick but very loud squawk and they instantly flew off of him and the other birds lowered their plumes as ordered.

Hazel reached up and brought the large bird into a warm embrace. She saw Hare watching. "This is the Umbrella clan. Harrison Hare, meet Bousteramah. Bousteramah, meet Mr. Harrison Hare of the Glade Territory!"

"Greetings Mr. Hare," said the huge bird.

"Nice to meet ya' Mr. Booster... Boosta-!"

"Just call me Rama. Nice to meet you too Mr. Hare. Any friend to Hazel-Mae is a friend to us." Rama then turned his attention to Hazel-Mae.

"We were the closest flock to you and have flown over the transport road. It doesn't look good; not from the air or ground. There's a significant portion of the gorge bridge missing."

Hazel got serious. "All of that debris had to fall on someone. This was always a threat. And the slingers; did you talk to Bopitallian?"

"No, didn't see any of the clan as we just did a quick fly over. We're here to assist you so I'll keep half the flock here and send the other half to see how the clan is doing."

"Thanks Rama but just leave two of your best scouts to assist us through the south forest."

“As you wish.”

“Thank you Rama. See you at the site”

Rama took off followed by the rest of the large flock minus two birds who perched on the ponies. Hazel still appeared to be worried but knew the slingers; unless some of them were caught in falling debris and swept into the chasm during the collapse, there would be no cause for concern.

Hazel whistled an odd string of notes as the two birds flew up to a nearby branch allowing them to saddle up. Hazel turned to Hare, “one bird will be perching on your shoulder and the other one on mine. Don't worry, these guys are our protectors and they've been instructed not to chew on your ears!”

Hare laughed, “Thank you for that! Much appreciated.”

After tightening straps and giving the ponies water, Hazel and Hare rode off toward the gorge with one bird each. Hare decided to practice and discovered this particular species of bird loves music! Hare continued to play while the bird bobbed it's head to the sound. Hare took a break for proper introductions.

Hare cleared his throat, “My name's Harrison Hare. What's yours?”

The bird's plume went up as he bobbed his head, “I am Scout 436. Hazel-Mae has Scout 784. Nice to meet you Mr. Hare. You have a nice trumpet there. Your center valve pad is slightly worn causing your note to be an eighth-step off. Might want to get that looked at.”

Hare looked astonished! “You know about trumpets? That's amazing!”

“I know about sound, Mr. Hare,” replied Scout 436.

Hare laughed too as he now had a new friend! Hare closely inspected the valves and noticed a tiny twig had been embedded in the pad. He picked it off and began playing again. Although he couldn't hear an interval that fine, when he saw Scout 436 with plume up flapping his large wings, he knew it was fixed! Hare audibly laughed as did Hazel-

Mae!

Hare wanted to show Scout 436 his fathers prized trumpet. He carefully pulled it out. “Listen to this one!”

Hare began playing while both birds were singing; and all four were laughing! You could see them clowning around with both scouts doing aerial acrobatics and singing to Hare's high notes!

At one point, Hare had doubled over the saddle of his pony because he was laughing so hard! They didn't have a long way to go before entering the dark South Coastal Forest but Hare was having too much fun and completely forgot to ask Scout 436 what it was like to fly!

As they approached the south forest, Hare slung the 'kick-around' bell over his shoulder using the strap he made instead of meticulously putting it away in it's case. Hazel noticed this but didn't give it a second thought since Hare would practice when the notion presented itself. The ponies slowed as they sat and assessed their position.

Hazel turned in her saddle and instructed Hare. “As I've mentioned, there are few problems in this forest because of the slingers but things may be different now. Due to damage we don't know without seeing it, certain animals may have been displaced meaning they've been forced out of their normal habitat and into foreign ones. We must proceed cautiously. We still have some distance to go and only four hours of daylight. The critical thing is to not stray from the road. It will be difficult to see at times but our scouts have much better eyesight in the dark than we do. Follow closely behind me Harry and we'll be there in no time. Master scouts, lead the way!”

Hare noticed that instantly both scouts raised their tall plumes but said nothing. This told Hazel they were ready. Since it was easier to speak their language, she made a few very rapid shrill calls and Scout 784 instantly flew off to map their way and communicate it back. Scout 436 remained as a deterrent since the Umbrella clan are aggressively fearless and tirelessly fierce when defending family and allies.

Hazel was actually very relieved to see the flock. With a large flock like Rama's, there isn't anything that can escape. Each bird has needle like talons, great strength and lift, and a vice-like strong razor sharp beak that can fell trees. As if that weren't enough natural defenses, these giant birds also possessed a decibel packed screech that can disorient even the largest animal and can be heard from great distances; and that was just one bird – Rama's air force numbered in the thousands.

Luckily, although the Coastal Transport Route was very old and worn, it had been maintained. That was only a small part of Hazel-Mae's important function in her territory; to observe and act if necessary. But, she had to know first. Thanks to Betzo, she did.

Hazel-Mae was hoping damage to the crossing wasn't as bad as described by Betzo and Rama. "Roughly forty feet" and "a significant portion" were vague accounts so she was hoping they exaggerated.

Just then, the shrill screech from scout 784 off in the distance was repeated by scout 436 sitting on Hare's shoulder.

"We're here! Slinger territory," announced Hazel-Mae.

Hare looked as far as the darkness would allow but only saw shadows of trees and large branches hanging down. He carefully followed Hazel as she turned left and proceeded through a narrow but thick passage. The old, dried out branches tore her gown and poked Hare but as soon as they squeezed through, they were blinded by sudden bright sunlight.

When their eyes adjusted finally, Hare was once again amazed! With several hundred of Rama's flock surrounding them up in the trees and elsewhere, there were also dozens of snakes simply dangling and hanging from the tree branches. Hazel-Mae looked around hoping to see Bopitallian.

They dismounted their ponies and walked into the forest of dangling snakes. Looking closer as his eyes adjusted more, Hare could now clearly see the community of snakes literally just hangin' around.

He turned to Hazel to ask her about them but before she could warn him to be quiet, it was too late. Hare successfully obliterated their peace and quiet making them drop from their dangling positions all at once and began heading straight toward him.

Hare's eyes widened as he backed up. He looked over at Hazel-Mae but she was around the corner talking to Rama. He couldn't back up anymore and wouldn't have time anyway. Before he knew it, they were on him.

Hare recalled Hazel telling him how these snakes can crush boulders but he soon discovered they were simply curious. He stood motionless as his new friends slithered around his long feet and started to coil around him which actually tickled.

Hare raised his arms in the air and yelled to Hazel, “what am I supposed to do here?”

Hazel turned and saw Hare's predicament. “Oh my,” she exclaimed laughing as she hurried over to Hare. “Follow me and they will follow you!”

Hare was allowed to be set free to walk and follow Hazel. She was right, whatever direction Hare went, they did also. This is when Hare's new large group of friends began asking questions, all at once:

“Ssso who are you?” one snake asked. Another asked, “where do you come from?” Then more questions were asked by the others; “What's hanging around your neck?” “Why are your feet so long?” “What's up with those ears?” “How old are you?” “Do you guys really eat carrots?”

“Sssssss!”

At once Hare's curious followers instantly ceased asking questions. Hazel looked around excited at hearing the loud hiss because she knew where it came from.

Hazel turned, and there was Bopitallian. Hare saw this snake rise up and curl around her so fast it only took a second. This scared Hare because it showed just how fast these creatures were. He didn't worry though because he knew this was a sign of affection.

“Bop,” exclaimed Hazel Mae! She could barely wrap her arms around the giant snake. “You look in very good health! Is everyone okay?”

“Dear Hazel,” said Bop as he unwound himself! “Yesss, we all are well but I've been afraid of this happening. It was only a matter of time.”

“Yes, I've expected it too.” She then turned to Hare. “Bopitallion, meet Harrison Hare of the Glade Territory. Harry, meet Master Slinger

Bop!"

"Nice to meet you Bop!"

"Good to meet you too Harry!"

"I just need to see what we're up against," said Hazel.

"You won't like it. Follow me and be careful of the edge," said Bop," those leaves and pine needles are slippery."

When they approached the site, Hazel-Mae was shocked to see the impossible mess this made, but was also relieved because Rama and Betzo did exaggerate, but just a bit. It hardly mattered though since unless you were a slinger or could fly, you would not be crossing this bridge.

Hazel stood there pondering the damage and appeared to Bop to be indecisive about what to do.

Bop wound his way back toward Hazel then quickly coiled himself so that he was face to face with her. "I have an idea that we've used in the past that will work."

"Please do tell," said Hazel.

Bopitallian called for a meeting between his three highest officers, Rezil, Grashe, Belfg. The four snakes, Rama, Hazel, and Hare stood looking at the center of the bridge where the massive chunk had been obliterated by the huge falling trees.

"What I propose," said Bop, "is that we simply make a bridge."

At first Hare acted as if it were a ridiculous idea but seconds later looking around at all the trees, he nodded his head in agreement. Bop watched his reaction and quickly coiled up to be face to face with him. "Not a bridge made from branches, but one made from usss!" Bop quickly stuck out his long forked-tongue and with a smile he said,"ssssso, here's what I propose." He then nodded to Rama.

Instantly Rama screeched out an order and within seconds all two hundred birds were gone. Hare stood wondering what was happening. Hazel knew where Bop was going with his idea...

“Harry,” explained Hazel, “what the birds are doing is stripping down wood posts long enough to traverse twice the width of the missing bridge. Once enough of them are in place, the snakes will crawl out on and around them and make an intertwined, braided, mesh type bridge across the gorge. Then we can cross and be on our way-”

Bop interjected, “-we've only used this method once but it worked. Unfortunately, repairing the bridge again won't be so easy or quick.”

Hare looked over at Hazel appearing unsure. She looked at him and put the ball in his court, “you decide! This is your musical quest Harrison Hare!”

“Don't have a choice,” said Hare. “How much daylight do we have?”

Hazel looked up and nodded, “about three hours.”

Hare nodded to Bop, “That sounds good to me. When do you think the birds will be back?”

Bop coiled then raised his body motioning in the northern-most direction, “you mean those birds?”

Hare turned and saw a massive wall of white seemingly floating toward them.

Just as the great white wall was approaching, instantly most of them landed and perched on something but only a few flew into position and placed the posts where they needed to be. And then just like Bop said, his fellow slingers made short work of intertwining themselves in and around each other to form a stable, though bumpy bridge. Hare just shook his head in amazement once again then turned to Hazel-Mae.

“Ladies first,” offered Hare as he swept the air with his arm!

“Why thank you Sir Harry, such a gentleman bunny! I'll lead the ponies across then it's your turn.”

“Ready-Rabbit! That's me!”

Hazel had already tied the ponies together and led them slowly, carefully, and successfully across. This took some time because although the ponies weren't afraid since they couldn't see the drop, it was the very uneven road made from big, round, snake bodies. The snake bridge was more than twelve feet wide so there was plenty of room so long as you proceeded slowly.

As soon as Hazel was standing on the other side, she yelled to Hare, "your turn Harry. Make sure those long feet don't trip you. Be careful!"

Hare yelled back, "yes, I will be v e r y careful."

Hare stepped on the snake bridge with one foot getting a feel for what he would have to walk on. He felt okay then stepped out and proceeded very slowly across the exact center of the bridge. Feeling more confidant and seeing the other side, he wanted to speed up but didn't risk it. Hare was planning every foot placement and every move.

Like we all do when trying to maintain balance, he was waving his arms around but his thumb caught on the shoulder strap hanging around his neck as his trumpet flew off into the gorge.

Instinctively Hare reached out to catch it but instead of his long foot getting caught in between the snakes, his heel slipped making him fall backwards.

Blind reaction then made him reach out for his trumpet in a futile last attempt as he rolled off the snake bridge and disappeared into the bottomless void of the gorge.

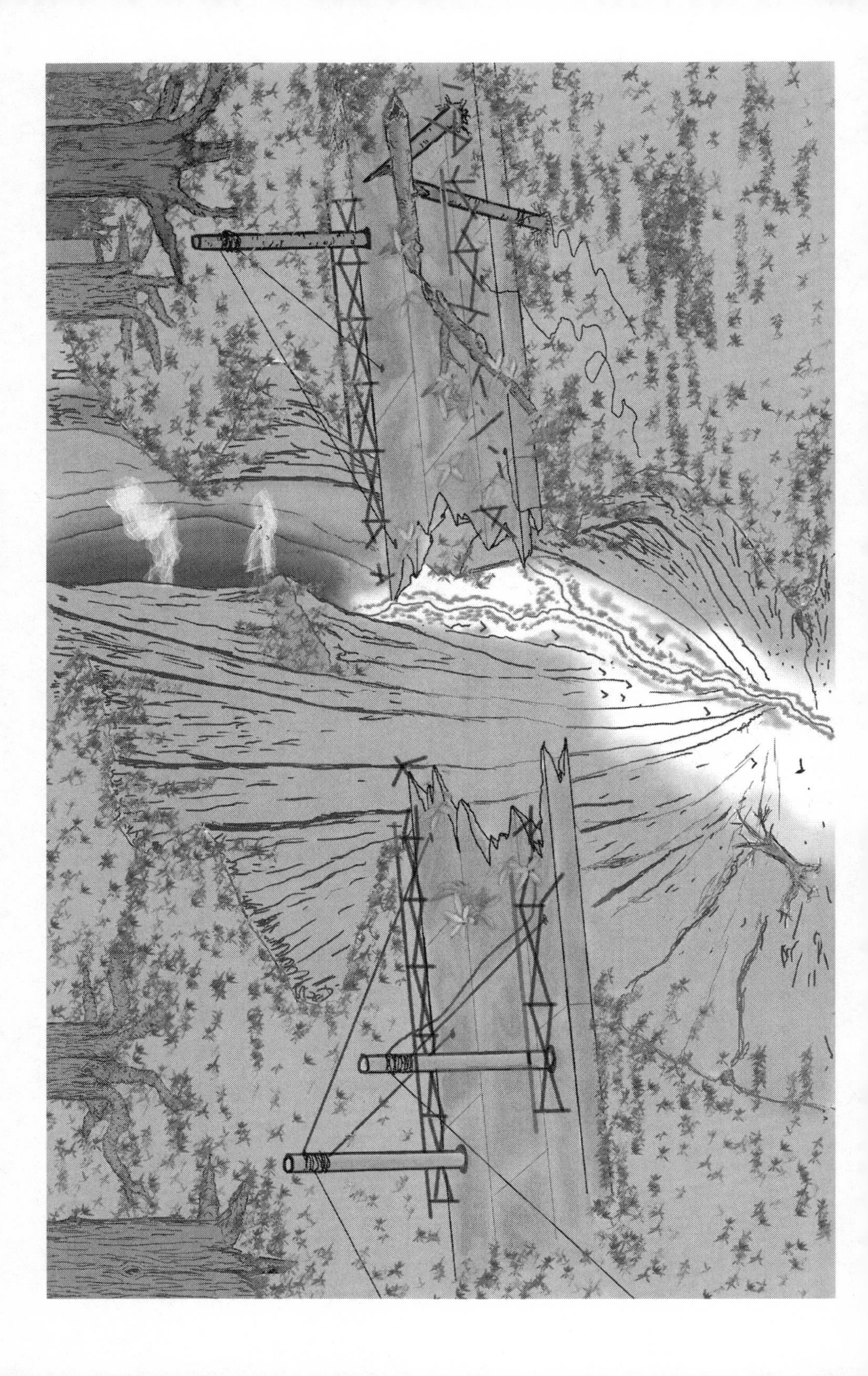

Chapter Five

Hazel-Mae screamed in disbelief as she fell to her knees. She covered her face with her hands and collapsed where she was, slumped over weeping repeating the word, “no, no, NO, NO-”

Neither clan had ever seen her vulnerability. No one ever had. The human girl side of the legend; the moment when the magical, all-knowing keeper of the territory wasn't invincible.

Rama's best fliers converged and flew into the gorge as Bop and several other of his most accomplished slingers coiled up as tightly as they could, then released the mainspring.

Bop had never been more determined. Nothing was more important than to save Hare.

Bop could see Hare flailing helplessly far below him through intermittent clouds and dozens of birds. Still, Bop kept his sharp eyes zeroed in on Hare.

Like a missile with scales, Bop was straight as an arrow. He sliced through the air past the birds and nearly had a collision but Rama's force were magical in flight. The other slingers planned to sling much deeper than Bop to hopefully secure lower areas in case there was a fall.

Bop continued to displace the air with his ever increasing speed and was confident because he often used this exact same sling-route during his competition practice. However catching a living thing moving erratically had never been done. But, the mark was fast approaching.

Bop knew every twig, branch, limb, or old tree trunk that protruded out from the gorge walls. There were many old oak trunks and large branches that would work but he had to get to Hare first and he had to get to him fast. He felt good about this because Hare was in clear view and his screaming was now clearly audible.

Bop flew past Hare preparing for the first stage of the sling. Hare was out of his mind as you could imagine and didn't even know Bop was there; to Hare he was going to die. When the timing was right, Bop slung his tail end toward the old stump sticking out and in a split second coiled tightly around it.

Having positioned himself properly, Hare just fell into his 'coil-range' where Bop simply coiled the upper half of his body around the falling Hare. It was quite a jolt for Hare being stopped so abruptly from such a long free fall but he was safe – for now.

While Bop was concentrating on whether the old rotted stump would hold their weight, Hare thought they were on the ground and began to celebrate.

Bop only needed to tighten his massive constrictor body gently around the tiny bunny and Hare calmed down instantly then came to his senses when he realized precisely where he was.

Rama had perched on the old stump right above Bop and looked down at him, "Hazel screams still..."

"Go protect and comfort her. I have this," commanded Rama.

"I will leave a squadron to-" Rama was cut off.

"No," repeated Bop sternly, "take your regiment and look after Hazel-Mae. We're going all the way to the bottom where there are razor-fly swarms that I'm sure you'd rather avoid. Instruct Rezil to take over for me and let our clan care for Hazel and her ponies. Send a company to her family in Brelojia. Make sure Hazel knows we will survive this and will send word when we are able. Go. Now!"

Rama bobbed his head then raised his tall plume and in seconds the Umbrella clan were on their way to help Hazel-Mae.

That left Bop and Hare dangling from only 75 feet which meant there was roughly 237 feet to go. Hare continued to be still since he couldn't see through the clouds but remained petrified with terror.

"I HATE THIS," screamed Hare!

Bop tried to intervene, "now is not the time to-"

".... all of this is because of me! Enough of this stupid musical quest. Get me back up to Hazel-Mae. Call the birds or do whatever you have to so we can stop this now."

As Bop slightly tightened his grip, Hare bit him which instantly made Bop nearly crush Hare who yelped-

There was a pause as Bop released his grip then instantly his menacing snake-face was literally nose to nose with Hare. There's something about being started down by an angry snake who's reptilian eyes are piercing yours who could crush you like a hollow log.

"It would take more than your weak bite to hurt me," scolded Bop, "instead of resorting to childish tantrums, you might consider becoming more part of the solution rather than intensifying the problem. I do have a solution but it's risky and you won't like it."

"I already don't like it," grumbled Hare.

"Good," answered Bop, "we are in agreement then because I don't like it either but no other options remain."

Hare remained in the tight grip of Bop but realized it was a much safer place to be than standing precariously on a thin ledge with no way up, around, or down.

"Okay," relented Hare, "I'm sorry I bit you. My life is in your hands and I am grateful."

"Apology accepted," Bop said while chuckling.

"What could possibly be amusing?" asked Hare.

"You said your life is in my hands... uhm, I have no hands... it was a joke. If you laugh you'll feel better, and feeling better is positive which we need right now."

Hare was still terrified but he ended up actually laughing a little, "not bad Bop. Thanks."

"Sssso, here's my plan."

Upon hearing Bop's plan, at first Hare thought it was insane, but yet he realized so was his current situation. But, there was something about it that Hare understood but wasn't yet clear. He definitely had to be on the same page as Bop though.

"So, before I attempt to fly, let me get this straight. You want me to jump off this ledge and head toward that huge branch way down there. Then you'll do your sling thing and hope to catch me, right? I did hear you right, right?"

"Yes. You heard me right."

"And if I miss?"

"Then you die," answered Bop, "and I would also."

Hare was silent for a moment rubbing his chin, thinking. He began to understand and was now nodding his head up and down.

"No, no wait I get it," said Hare excited, "you've already proved what you can do because we're alive. I should have and would have been dead but I get it. Since you can fall much faster then me and can also control your direction, we simply do the same thing again!"

'Yesss," replied Bop, "but anything over twenty feet is a long drop and you don't weigh much. Without some form of propulsion, you'd drop like a stone. And there isn't enough ledge to push off from-"

"......unless you're a rabbit! So, you've never seen a rabbit hop? Or how a rabbit can jump when we need to? Look at my huge feet! You aren't very bunny savvy are you? "said Hare almost laughing.

Bop smiled sensing him relax, "no, no I suppose I'm not. So you say you can launch yourself from where you're standing far enough for me to have a good shot at catching you?"

"Sure can but that won't be enough," deduced Hare, "but, if you can sling yourself like that you can certainly sling me too right?"

Hare saw Bop liking his idea and continued while clapping his hands, "okay then Boppo, how about this? I stand on the tip of your tail while holding on to you. Just when we're ready, I jump at the same time as you sling me. That should do it.... so long as you don't sling me into that side of the mountain over there!"

Bop found a brand new respect for Hare although he tried not to show it. Hare not only took control of the dire situation and in fact solved their problem but also obliterated his fear by facing it.

Now, they just had to live through it.

"Okay, I'm impressed! Nice job you nut, "said Bop smiling, "it's just crazy enough to work!"

"Only one way to find out," said Hare.

"Ready?" asked Bop.

"Yeah, give me a few seconds to picture this," said Hare as he closed his eyes. He was slowly waving his arms and Bop saw his ears gyrate in different positions. A few more seconds elapsed when he opened his eyes. "Okay," said Hare concentrating more than he ever had, "let's go on four. So I'll count, one, two, three, then BAM, I'm flying. And I aim for that big branch, right?"

"Yesss. Timing is the critical thing but let me worry about that," said Bop. "Trust that I will catch you."

"I trust you Bop," replied Hare trying to smile.

"Okay, this is it, man," said Hare. "Ready Bop?"

"Ready."

"One, two, three, and..." Hare was slung like an arrow toward the side of the mountain but just when he thought he might collide with it, he felt himself falling. Without even trying, his long ears and feet automatically adjusted to where he needed to go and actually did help him keep a somewhat sufficient course hopefully long enough for Bop to do what he needed to.

Just then, Bop shot past him like a rocket and used his slinky snake body to do exactly what he did before. This time though, Hare could see it.

No sooner did Bop's head pass over the huge branch, his body instantly coiled around it. Hare could clearly see where he needed to land. He was a little off which meant Bop had to really stretch to be able to coil around him properly, but it worked.

Hare's tiny body was curled up in a very strong cocoon so fast his head spun.

They both didn't move, didn't breath, but waited. Then waited some more. They smiled at each other thinking they had this but then they heard one root break, then a few others, then...

Hare knew what was happening and didn't waste time closing his eyes in fear. Instead he was looking down searching for their next stop. “There! That big oak way down there.”

“Yesss, perfect scope,” said Bop. “As soon as this branch separates, I'll push off strong then straighten out. As soon as we're over that oak I'll coil again. You hang on as tight as you can because this will be a bumpy ride.”

“Don't worry about me,” replied Hare loudly, “let's get to solid ground!”

“I hear that brother,” answered Bop!

The rotted branch took time to separate itself but finally did. As soon as it was free, Bop pushed off with just enough force to line themselves up with the large oak Hare saw.

They fell freely and very calmly but the more terminal velocity that built up, the harder their landing on the old oak would be – then the same thing would happen as the branch breaking loose.

“We're going to hit hard, hang on,” shouted Bop!

“I'm-ready-for-it...” yelled Hare.

When they landed on the huge, dead oak tree, luck was with them as the oak did break off and seemed to provide a perfect vehicle for a bumpy but safe cushioned ride all the way to ground.

Bop turned over so the armor-like scales on his back would not allow splintered tree branches to impale his vulnerable underside. He also curled Hare into himself more securely to protect him also.

They were now accelerating quickly as the old dry leaves from the dead tree were stripped off so no leaf cushion remained.

Hare was able to see the ground rushing toward them as he clenched his teeth.

Chapter Six

Not many know what may lie, crawl, or ooze, at the bottom of Snake Gorge. Although the slinger snakes venture down into the dark depths occasionally, they never had a reason to stay.

Why anyone would choose to reside in this very dark and bleak place would be anyone's guess. Luckily though, one creature loved it.

Trobanturnariac, or Troby is one of the last cave dwelling Buffarilla species still living. Being half Gorilla and half Buffalo, he stood just slightly less than nine feet tall and his brute strength has never been measured. Fortunately, Troby's species wasn't threatened with extinction but he is one of the few as his brethren are widely scattered except for one.

So, despite Bop and Hare's serious predicament, they were incredibly lucky. Troby was just around the bend gathering firewood when they fell from the sky landing with a sound Troby could have heard back in his cave.

Troby ignored the sound at first since things were thrown into the abyss all the time but this sound was not just debris; he sensed it then smelled it.

By the time he got to where Hare and Bop landed he saw them intertwined within the broken branches and limbs. Hare was hurt and not able to stand and Bop had been pinned down by the large trunk and wasn't moving.

Seeing their predicament, Troby rushed over to Hare and asked, “are you okay? No broken bones?”

Hare looked up at the towering monster and said with effort, “no broken bones, thank you. Please tend to my friend. His name is-”

“-Bopitallian,” said Troby as he let out a very deep and sinister sounding laugh. “Yeah, I know Bop the snake.” Troby said gruffly and began lumbering slowly toward the helpless Bop turning his huge head one way then the other deeply humming to himself.

Hare was instantly gripped with fear beyond falling to his death. Troby was an absolute missing link and it appeared to Hare that Bop had a very formidable enemy.

Troby continued to slowly pace around the trapped snake singing, “snake, snake, snake, oh the meal you'll make. Ah yes, the slinger who silently slithers and sneaks down here into my domain to steal from me. I knew one day this would happen and I've been waiting for it. Oh, and the other slingers you sent down to fend me off will make a good meal too. Retribution for stealing my food.”

Troby reaching down to grab Bop as Hare struggled to do something to help the one who saved him. Troby turned quickly and yelled so loudly Hare cringed, “I can crush you like a bug. Then I will add you to my dinner as well.”

Hare wasn't sure what to do or how to respond. Exhausted, and injured, he simply passed out from his pain and trauma falling back against the tree trunk.

The savory smell of some sort of delicious stew or soup boiling made Hare wake up quickly. Thinking he was dreaming, he opened his eyes only to see himself in a large well lit cave. The fireplace flickered with a large crackling fire sending shadows dancing off the uneven rock walls. The fireplace reminded him of not only Brax's cave, but his as well. He then struggled to move, grunting in pain.

Troby heard him and walked over as Hare crouched helplessly thinking the boiling cauldron he saw was for him. Troby laughed and put his mind at ease, “look who's awake? How ya doin'?” Troby moved closer to check Hare out but he backed up terrified.

Troby wondered what was up with Hare. He held up his huge arms and said, “what's your problem? I'm not going to hurt you.”

“What you said about Bop. What you said about crushing me like a bug. I will fight if I have to...”

“Hold up there pal. I motioned to you indicting that I was going to play a joke on that crazy slinger. If you didn't see it, that is not my problem. So, don't worry I'm not going to stomp on you and Bop is fine. Wow...maybe I *should* move. The weird stuff that falls from up there just will not stop.”

Hare stammered still sizing up the situation...“so, we're cool?”

Troby let out a loud belly laugh, “Of course! I gotta say, this cracks me up because ol' Bop and me go way back and he's done a lot of crazy things but never anything like this!”

Hare was relieved to say the least, but that didn't make his leg feel any better. He sat up as much as he could and began grumbling to himself, “my leg is probably broken. This is just great-”

“Your leg isn't broken,” said Troby looking at the wound,” it feels like it but its just a bruised bone or a sprain. You'll be okay but it'll take some time.”

Just then the other two slingers that followed Bop into the gorge, Grashe and Belfg, approached Hare. “Our Master is resting but asked us to relay to you he is fine and will be moving around soon. Thank you.” With that, they both side-winded their way off to where Bop was being tended to.

Troby was stirring the concoction boiling in the cauldron and looked over at Hare, “I gotta ask ...how in the world did you end up down here in paradise? Those crazy slinger snakes talk you into taking a ride on the wild side?”

“No,” said Hare, “those crazy slingers snakes saved my life... well Bop did anyway.”

“Oh man, I can't wait to hear this story,” laughed Troby while tasting his broth. “Now that is a perfect batch! Here, have some of this, it'll help you heal. Careful, it's very hot!” Troby spooned out a bowl full and handed it to Hare.

Hare thanked him and didn't hesitate eating something hot or not. He carefully sipped the spoonful and looked up at Troby who smiled complimenting himself, “not bad grub for a big, hairy beast huh?”

“This is really, really good,” said Hare gently blowing on his spoonful.

“Well, I guess it doesn't matter how you got down here or why,” said Troby taking a bite of bread, “the question would be, where were you going and what are your plans now?"

"I'll tell you in a minute... this is s o good!"

"Okay, you enjoy. I'll go check in on Bop."

Troby walked away and Hare was mad since he couldn't get up and walk around. Now that he knew he was in good hands, he continued to enjoy the hot food. Just then Troby returned and noticed he finished his bowl. "Want some more?"

Hare nodded and held up the bowl, "yes please! That soup is excellent. What is it?"

"It's not soup. It's stew. Rabbit stew," said Troby looking very serious as if the cauldron was meant for him after all.

Hare remembered all the jokes played on him when he was younger and wasn't going to bite. Hare took the bowl from him deciding to play along. He sipped from his spoon again and looked up at Troby, "hmmm, you know, this broth would be excellent for rabbit stew, but like duck, rabbit tends to be too greasy."

Troby busted up laughing because he thought he had Hare going there for a minute!

"Hey, Harry, get over here!" Belfg yelled from around the corner. Not thinking, Hare actually jumped up and walked a few steps before the pain reminded him. He stopped and tried to limp.

Hare looked over at Troby, "hey, I think I can walk!"

"Hey, I think you're nuts," corrected Troby, "you're going to aggravate it and make it worse." Troby looked around and then turned to Hare, "wait one minute-"

Troby walked over into another part of the cave and quickly returned with a sturdy old dried tree branch that would serve as a cane. He handed it to Hare, "here, use this until I find something better; and be careful cruising around. That stick can slide on this stone floor."

Hare wasn't worried about a little pain, he just wanted to say hello to his awesome new friend. He slowly limped his way across the floor, and around the corner where there were some rock steps that were difficult to manage but he did. Troby wanted to simply pick him up and carry him but knew Hare at least had to exercise his wound slowly for it to heal.

Once Hare reached the top of the steps, he could see Bop laid out straight on top of a stone slab with blankets under him. Hare saw blood and rushed over to him stumbling, almost dropping his cane.

“Bop! Bop, you're bleeding!” Hare instantly looked over at Troby with a frantic look on his face. “Will he be okay?”

Troby shook his head not up and down or even side to side; it was an unsure gesture. “He was sliced pretty badly, and punctured in places. I can patch you up if you have a small cut or help someone with a hurt leg but I'm no doctor.”

“I'll be fine,” said Bop with difficulty. “Earlier Grashe and Belfg went for cinder-moss and raspfern root mud. It's our typical remedy for cuts and pokes but I feel it working, and like your leg, it will just take time. I wanted to know how you were Harry.”

Hare limped closer to Bop and gently petted his hand over him. He had never felt a snake before and was amazed at how armor-like but smooth their scales were. Hare felt tears welling up, “how can I possibly thank you for saving my life. You put your life on the line to save me when you didn't even know me; all because of a stupid trumpet. I wish I never had it-”

“Trumpet?” Troby looked at Hare, “that trumpet is yours!?”

Hare quickly looked up at Troby, “you found my trumpet?!!?”

“Wow, pretty excited for a stupid trumpet you wish you never had,” said Troby smiling at Hare. “yeah, I can only assume it's yours because I can guarantee you there ain't nothing living down here that plays anything. I'll be right back.”

Troby walked away and Hare couldn't believe it. With everything that had taken place Hare realized he hadn't even thought about it. Troby soon returned with Hare's trumpet showing a decent sized dent in the bell and a broken shoulder strap. He handed it to Hare who dropped his cane and pain or no pain, did his happy-bunny-dance!

Hare started playing and Troby was shaking his head up and down thinking he was pretty good. Just when Troby was going to comment on Hare's playing, he abruptly stopped; no speech, no expression...

He let Hare play a few seconds longer then interrupted him, "Hey pal. Please stop playing."

By now, Hare was able to hobble around the flat gallery playing but then stopped and looked over at Troby who's expression was blank. Hare added it up then slowly looked over at Bop.

The master slinger snake whom he had just met and who had saved his life was dead.

Chapter Seven

Hare's ears instantly drooped as his horn hit the ground with a metallic clanking sound that eerily echoed throughout the cavern. Hare lowered his head and began to weep.

Both Belfg and Grashe coiled around him because they felt the connection between their late Master and Hare. Troby walked over and sat with them putting his massive arm around Hare's shoulder.

For a very long time no one made a sound.

Finally, Troby broke the silence by grunting and slowly getting up. Hare sniffled then managed to croak out a question, "where are you going?"

"Soup might burn," said Troby who didn't have the usual brisk step in his walk. As he walked toward the cauldron, he angrily kicked a stone on the ground that went shooting across the stone floor.

After making sure he wouldn't burn up a brand new batch of food, he silently stood watching Hare who sat head in hands, immobile. Finally knowing that Hare was now experiencing perhaps the first serious guilt-trip in his young life, Troby intervened.

"Harry," began Troby. "I think-"

"No, Troby," interrupted an angry Hare, "I know what you're going to say and you'd be wrong because this IS my fault, and I-"

"YES IT IS YOUR FAULT," roared Troby. "IS THAT WHAT YOU WANT TO HEAR?" The huge beast stood glaring down at Hare who wasn't sure what to expect.

Hare stared wide-eyed up at Troby who sighed heavily. He lowered his tone to nearly a whisper as he sat down next to him, "so, what now? Are you going to mope around feeling sorry for yourself? Do you expect me to coddle you and lie saying this was not your fault and everything will be alright? Well guess what, I won't do that because fault doesn't matter. Bad stuff happens dude. It was an accident. Besides what's done is done and it cannot be undone...so now you must accept the reality and deal with it."

Troby sat watching Hare waiting for any form of rebuttal... there was none so he continued...

"Let's talk honestly," said Troby. "Bop would have eventually died slinging anyway trying to save you or not. It's a very dangerous game because if you miss, you die; it's just that simple. I've always said he took too many chances. Well, think of it like this... his last sling not only made his name immortal, which he would have loved, but saved you in the process. So, if any good can come from this, that's it. Besides, to repeat myself, since you can't change it, your only move is to move forward."

Finally, Belfg and Grashe who rarely spoke, approached Hare and Troby; Belfg spoke first, "Bopitallian was our leader and friend. He was always fair and truly cared and I hate to admit it but Trobanturnariac is right, he took way too many chances. We all worried about it... he will be missed tremendously."

"Hazel-Mae always said so too," said Grashe as his snake snout pointed toward Hare and Troby saw it, "she'll be sad to hear he's gone. Don't forget she thinks you're gone too Mr. Hare."

Troby jumped to his feet startling everyone, "Hazel-Mae was with you?"

"Well, yeah," answered Hare, "she saw me go over and thinks I'm dead unless we can get word to her somehow."

Troby instantly looked over at Belfg and Grashe, "is she with your clan?"

"Yesss she is," replied Grashe, "Bousteramah's quarter flock is with us too."

"Good," replied Troby. "I'll find out what's really going on in a minute."

He then turned his attention to Hare and got serious. "Okay, so Bop saved you but why were you *and* Hazel-Mae up there in the first place? I've had this odd curiosity gnawing at me... anyone would expect to see Hazel-Mae occasionally since this is her province but a trumpet playing rabbit somehow doesn't fit. Want to shed some light on that?"

"Hazel-Mae and I were... *are* on a journey to a place called Rhythm Creek to meet up with a chimpanzee band."

Troby's eyes widened as he stammered, "Rhythm Creek huh? Hmm, never heard of it."

"It's supposed to be near Cedar Forest I think," replied Hare.

"Cedar Forest?" Troby pointed toward the cave entrance, "that's way over in that direction."

There was a pause in the conversation as Troby was thinking... "well alright, whatever but still, how did you end up down here in the lap of luxury?"

"The transport route bridge was destroyed by falling oaks or something like that and the snakes formed a bridge out of themselves and I tired to cross it and fell. Then.... Bop saved me and here we are. Now if we could..."

"I've been hearing more falling debris," said Troby rubbing his chin and ignoring Hare. "You have to expect that living down here especially with the recent storms. I'm always finding stuff people toss over the crossing up there, like your trumpet. I guess they like to see things disappear through the clouds. So, the crossing road is gone... that explains a lot."

Hare was becoming impatient, "it's very important to somehow send word to Hazel to let her know about Bop and me. If I have to I'll climb back up myself and..."

"Okay, okay, relax. Don't get bent. Give me a minute."

Troby walked off into another room and returned carrying several hollowed out logs of different sizes. After a few trips, he set them all up in a specific order just outside the caves entrance. Troby grabbed a few mallets and proceeded to drum out some complicated rhythms. He stopped then listened, then repeated drumming out more different combinations and stopped, listening.

This went on for a while when he finally put down the mallets and just stood there waiting.

Hare grew even more impatient, “so, what's going on?”

“Would you please be quiet?” Troby whispered to Hare.

There was silence for a while until way off in the distance Hare heard a series of faint sounds as if someone was tapping a stone against rock. It intensified as many other tapping sounds joined in. Before long there was a concert of various rhythms all intertwining and melding together echoing between the canyon walls. Then just as quickly, it all stopped at the same time.

Troby nodded while picking up the mallets answering. Hare was truly impressed! He never heard of percussive communication before and thought he'd like to learn it one day. Finally Troby stopped, hung the mallets on the hook, and calmly sat down.

Hare stood shaking his head, “so, what's going on?”

“What's going on is we wait.”

Hare immediately began pacing really showing his impatient side now. Before too long, small Plumeria flowers with tiny pebbles tied to their stalks slowly appeared drifting down from above landing softly upon the ground before them.

“There you go! See how easy that was? Hazel is on her way. Therefore Mr. Nut-bunny, you need to relax and rest that leg. No doubt as soon as Hazel gets here, you'll be back on the road.”

“I hope so.” Hare looked over to where Bop's lifeless body still lay wrapped in a blanket. “I'm sorry Bop. I will never forget, thank you.”

Troby walked over to Hare placing his hand on his shoulder, “Grashe and Belfg will take Bop back home in a little while. We have other slingers on their way.”

“Good. I'm glad to hear that. How long until Hazel gets here?” asked Hare.

Troby thought for a moment, “I'd estimate tomorrow around this time."

"That's kind of late in the day," said Hare, "she's not traveling alone is she?"

"Not a chance," responded Troby, "she'll have a platoon of slingers escorting her not to mention a good number of those crazy birds."

"Good to know," whispered Hare under his breath.

Hare and Troby sat in silence with Hare just staring at Bop's long body lying in state. He was grappling with the guilt he knew he'd have to eventually face when he looked over and saw his trumpet lying on the ground where he dropped it. He walked over and picked it up studying the damage and without warning Hare raised the trumpet above his head and slammed it down on the stone table Bop was lying on.

It's not easy to startle a monster like Troby but Hare succeeded. Even Grashe and Belfg jumped. Troby rushed over and tried to grab the trumpet out of Hare's hand before he swung it down again but Hare was too quick and pulled it away from him. "What are you doing?!!?"

"I'm done with this stupid horn, man. It's caused nothing but trouble...you said it yourself, a trumpet playing rabbit somehow doesn't fit." Hare held the trumpet by the mouthpiece, yelled and threw it out the cave entrance as it twirled through the air slamming against a tree. "That's it."

"NO," roared Troby making Hare run for cover, "that is NOT it!" Troby glared over at Hare who was seeing him really furious for the first time. Moving toward Hare, instead of walking around the solid tree stump he used for a table, he picked it up as if it weighed nothing and threw it halfway across the gallery. Hare was trembling now as Troby blocked the cave's entrance so he couldn't escape. Troby would never actually hurt Hare but at this moment Hare wouldn't bet on it.

Troby continued to roar at him, "so, Bop died for nothing? Is that what you're telling me? My friend for longer than two of your miserable lifetime's is dead because of you and your best idea is to just give up? I'll throw your fuzzy butt into that stew pot before I allow you to give up."

Hare lowered his guard and relaxed allowing his ears to droop.

Troby joined him as he leaned back against the cold stone wall as his back slid down it coming to rest on the ground. He didn't say anything for a while and didn't look over at Troby, but just stared over at Bop.

"I suddenly feel so lost. The worst thing I've ever done is swipe a turnip from that old cranky raccoon when I was little." Hare leaned up against him. "Now someone lost their life because of me. How can I possibly live with this guilt?"

"That's an easy one," Troby said giving him a friendly nudge, "just let it go by making Bop's death count by never giving up. Even if this never happened, you must never give up no matter how much pain it will cause you. Ask Hazel-Mae, she'll be the first one to agree."

Hare then stood up and walked with purpose over the scattered debris that used to be neatly placed as he said back to Troby, "Bop did not die in vain, and I promise that." He walked outside where the bright moonlight allowed him to easily locate his crumpled trumpet. He brought it back looking at it carefully.

Troby was watching him as he walked closer. "Bring that thing over here."

Hare handed the trumpet to Troby then sat down next to him. Troby held it up inspecting it then slowly looked down at Hare, "for a little bunny you can do some damage. Look at this thing! Here's a little shred of advice, don't take your guilt out on the horn, let the horn take that guilt out of you."

"Exactly right. All I've managed to do is destroy one of my father's trumpets. Now I'm making things worse."

"Hmm, well, I don't think it's destroyed," said Troby, "looks like this part here is the only thing bent. What do you call this?" asked Troby pointing to the front of the trumpet.

Hare chuckled, "that's the bell."

"Okay, the bell appears to be the only thing damaged. I can fix that," said Troby as he used his huge, strong fingers to gently push out the inward bends of the bell. When he was done he handed it to Hare. "Well, it still looks beat up but at least it's better. Try it out; you sounded pretty good before."

Hare took the trumpet and held it up, "thanks, I appreciate that." Hare played a few riffs and held notes that didn't waver. He fiddled around with the valves and everything was in working order. He lowered the horn, thought for a second, then slowly looked back up at Troby.

"You know what," said Hare, "you are a really good drummer. Your logs are still set up so lets jam a little!"

Troby laughed, "are you serious? I'm no drummer, I just communicate that way."

"All the more reason to lean toward music-". Hare was interrupted by a large group of slinger snakes entering Troby's cave led by Grashe and Belfg.

"We are here to take our Master home," said Belfg.

Hare was the first to get up as Troby was right behind him.

Unknown to Hare, Grashe and Belfg had already prepared Bop's long body by forming it into a circular coil which they tied with palm strands. This would make it easy to pass him up from the bottom of the gorge to their forest den.

The snakes performed a sad and unusual ceremony Hare couldn't understand as he stood with hands folded in front of him, sniffling throughout. Afterwards, in the hazy moonlight, Bop was pulled up one snake at a time until he disappeared into the forest ceiling high above them. Grashe and Belfg remained so as to greet Hazel-Mae and their fellow brethren when they would arrive sometime tomorrow. They both took refuge outside to keep watch.

Once again, Hare and Troby shared a meal in practically total silence until one by one, they both fell asleep.

Chapter Eight

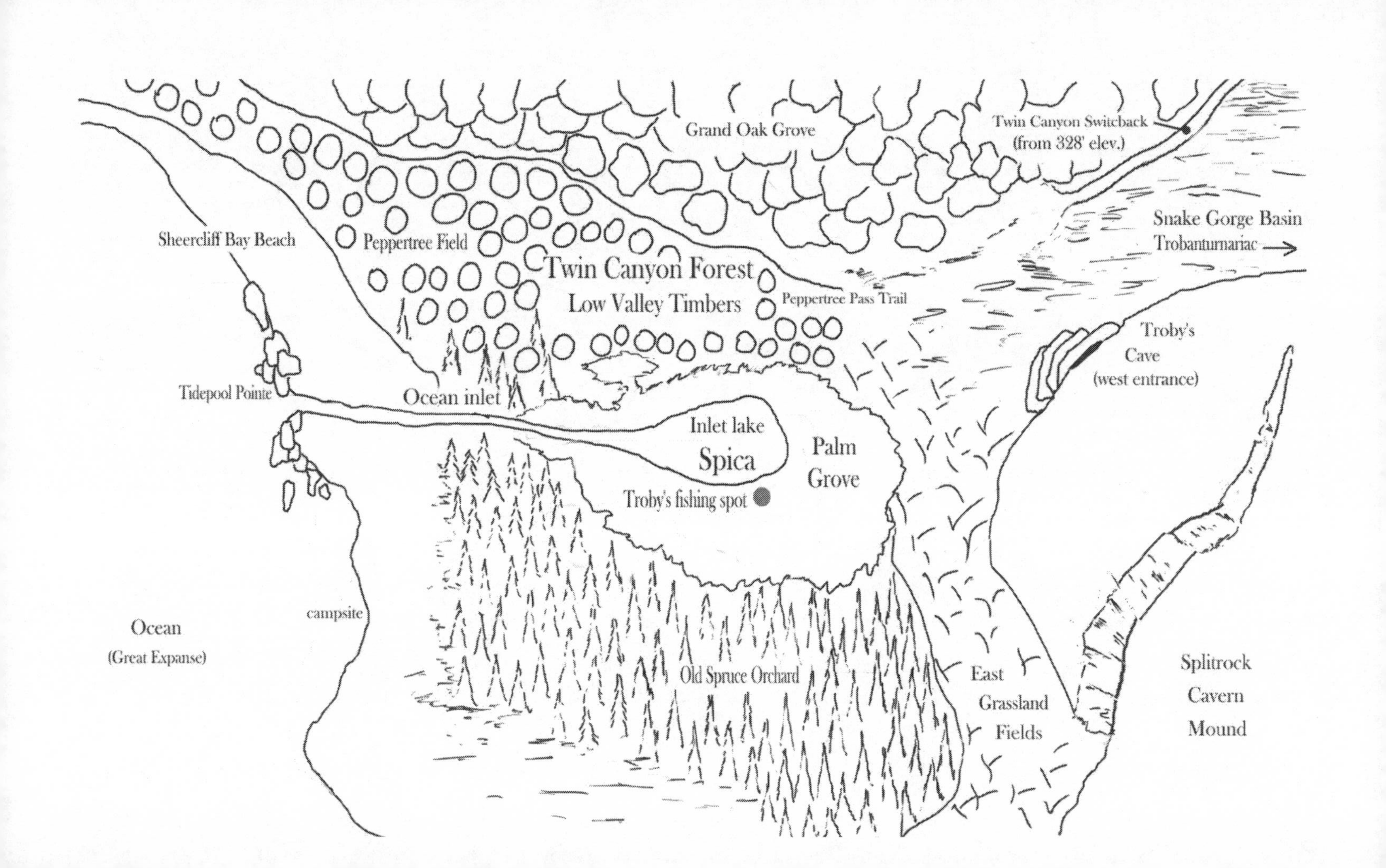
Grand Oak Grove
Twin Canyon Switchback
(from 328' elev.)
Snake Gorge Basin
Trobanturnariac →
Sheercliff Bay Beach
Peppertree Field
Twin Canyon Forest
Low Valley Timbers
Peppertree Pass Trail
Troby's
Cave
(west entrance)
Tidepool Pointe
Ocean inlet
Inlet lake
Spica
Palm
Grove
Troby's fishing spot
campsite
Ocean
(Great Expanse)
Old Spruce Orchard
East
Grassland
Fields
Splitrock
Cavern
Mound

For Hare, the morning was a loud and rude awakening due to Troby crashing around as if desperately trying to find something. While rubbing his eyes, Hare noticed it was still dark outside...

"Oh man," said Hare yawning, "the sun's not even up. What could you possibly be looking for?"

"My small fishing pole."

Hare never got out of bed so fast! He jumped up quickly not even noticing his leg didn't hurt as much!

"Let me help you look for it!"

Troby laughed noticing his exuberance, "aren't *we* in a good mood today? You must really love to fish.
"

"Oh yeah! I've only tried once but maybe I'll catch something this time!"

Troby slowly looked over at him astonished, "you've only gone fishing once?"

"Well, yeah. Back home, Round Rock Creek is my hangout but I never fished there. Actually my very first time fishing was a few days ago in Brelojia."

Troby nodded, "so you have never caught a fish..... ever?"

"Nope."

"Wow, really? Well, you're in luck because we are going to the inlet lake not far from here and the fish are always biting. Something about those salt-water fish, man! They'll strike at-"

"-salt water?" Hare asked curiously. "There's a salt water lake in the middle of the forest down here at the bottom of Snake Gorge?"

"Sure is," replied Troby pointing. "the ocean is roughly five or so miles in that direction."

Hare was really confused now. "Okay, wait. So two days ago I was body-surfing in Brelojia, now, you're telling me that after falling for over 300 feet there's another ocean way down here? How is that even possible?"

"You're asking me? I'm just a big hairy beast and don't know about irregular topography, subduction zones, or tectonic plate movements but I do know fishing. So, let's get going unless there are more questions."

"No, no," said Hare chuckling, "I thought after being swallowed by the earth, I'd never see the ocean again. But... okay, whatever you say pal! Let's go fishing!"

"Yeah, this whole region is unstable if you ask me. Anyway, the deal with the inlet lake is that the terrain moves in a gradual downward slope so we have a long, narrow, salt water river that empties out to form a lake. The fish that end up there are hungry since there aren't many critters for them to feed on. So, be prepared to catch your very first fish quickly and, chances are it'll be bigger than you!"

This made Hare dance around as much as he could. "Hey, bring it on! Watch me catch an awesome dinner for us and Hazel-Mae."

Troby laughed and nudged Hare, "I'll just bet you will!"

Hare helped Troby collect everything they needed and was now hopping around like a kid on Christmas morning!

"Okay," said Troby as they were about to leave, "I have the poles, the club, and my lucky fishing cap...."

"...and I have the tackle box, bota-bag with the good water, and a chub of dried meat for lunch," answered Hare excited! "Let's get going!"

They exited Troby's cave at the west entrance which opened up to the beautiful East Grassland Fields instead of the other entrance Hare knew all too well! The sun was just rising and the morning butterflies that swarmed around the fields were countless. Hare had to laugh because Troby was so tall, his entire head was covered with butterflies!

They didn't have to walk far to be clear of the butterfly cloud as they entered the palm groves of the twin canyon forest.

"So," asked Hare, "there are actually fish big enough to where you need a club to knock them out?"

Troby had to chuckle, "...ohhhh yes! The really super huge monster fish can't fit down the inlet but every once in a while, a beast-fish squeezes through. But even smaller fish will fight like crazy once you hook them. Then as soon as you get them on land they're flippin' and floppin' so one quick whap, and they go to sleep with no pain. Knocking out a beast fish is a much different matter."

Hare thought for a moment, "how do you know fish don't feel pain?"

"Well, for one thing they don't have the necessary brain power. Mainly though, they fight like crazy not because of pain but to get away from what ever is holding them, like your hook."

"...and how big is a beast-fish?" asked Hare curiously.

Troby rubbed his chin, "hmmm... see that huge boulder right there? From that size down to my size."

Hare looked up at Troby, "wow, seriously? Why bother with clubs, can't you just punch them out or something?"

Troby laughed, "yeah, right!!! Just punch out an 300 pound giant sea bass or a thirty foot barracuda with teeth longer than your trumpet; that wouldn't be my first choice for a good idea! Actually, a giant sea bass would be a first here but the barracuda's are long and narrow and can easily end up swimming down the inlet only to end up here."

Hare was intrigued, "and if I catch a big barracuda?"

"If you tangle with a barracuda over two feet, you'll need me to take over. But hey, let's just get started and see what happens!"

"Sound like a plan to me."

Our fearless anglers proceeded through the Canyon Forest with all of their gear swinging back and forth as they stepped over fallen logs and walked through tall reeds.

“We're getting close, “alerted Troby, “there's the slime! Be careful, it's slippery.”

Hare was now wondering how to clean all the bright green slime off of his feet when he heard the gulls cry. “Hey there's a seagull, we must be-”

With Hare's next breath a large clearing opened up like a huge gateway taking them from oaks and pepper trees to a thick orchard of palms. Through that was a large body of water that Hare thought would be smaller.

“Wow, this is no lake! We're at the ocean,” said Hare.

“It looks like it from where we're standing,” motioned Troby, “but this is actually a very small body of water but large enough to attract, or rather trap some really big fish.”

Hare looked up at Troby, “trap?”

“Well yeah, like I said, the inlet is a downward path so the water moves down carrying the fish that end up in the lake. Some are able to swim back out but most can't so they're easily caught or die being eaten by other critters. There's a constant flow of new sea water as the old water evaporates being replaced by the new.”

Hare rubbed his chin and said,” I've been seeing some pretty awesome places on this journey of mine but this is really cool! So where's this favorite spot you were bragging about?”

“Not far my friend, not far at all!”

They continued walking carefully due to the slippery moss when they finally arrived at a small beach with flat sand and plenty of room to catch dinner! Before Hare knew it, he was sitting next to Troby on a log learning how to fish.

“There are lots of fancy gizmo's some people use for tackle but I keep it simple because it works,” instructed Troby as he opened the tackle box. “Also, I rarely use bait because it's not needed, not here anyway. The fish in this lake will strike at anything that moves so don't go swimming because you'll most likely become bait.”

"I will definitely remember that, but how do you catch fish without bait?"

"We use this," said Troby as he held up an item Hare had never seen. "This is what is called a lure. See how it looks like a real fish with this three-prong hook hiding down here? Come over here and watch this."

Hare was excited because he had never received lessons in fishing and he was anxious to get started!

"There are many different knots used to secure your line to the hook, or swivel, or in our case, a lure," said Troby holding it up. "When that big, beautiful, hungry fish hits your line the knot has to hold up otherwise you're out one lure and go home hungry. This is the only knot I use so watch closely."

Troby's huge fingers looked to Hare as if they were too big to thread the line through the lure's eye, but he did it with ease. "Okay, see how I ran the line through twice? You take this end and wrap it around the main line five or six times. Then you take this end and pass it back through the double loops, add a little spit to moisten the line, and pull tight. Done! Now you try."

Hare practiced a few times and finally held up his fourth try and showed it to Troby who inspected it, nodded, patted Hare on the back and said, "good work, that looks perfect. Check out how strong that is!"

Troby didn't have the proper reels for long distance casting, so he had to show Hare how to use a basic reel to cast without turning it into an impossibly tangled mess. This took some time but finally after several frustrating tries, Hare was confident and ready to catch his very first fish.

"Okay," instructed Troby, "when a fish hits, be patient then set the hook by pulling up quickly then yank that big plateful right out of the water!"

"....or the plateful pulls me in, then I become dinner, right?" asked Hare.

Troby stammered a bit, "uhmm, well, yeah... that's always a possibility here, that's why I told you about the beast fish. But cast into shallow water where the smaller fish are. I'll wrestle with the big one's."

"Okay, I'm ready-rabbit," exclaimed Hare enthusiastically, "dinner, here we come!"

Nearly an hour went by and they didn't get so much as a nibble. Troby was annoyed because he wanted to prove to Hare he wasn't just talk. Hare didn't mind because he was just having fun... but still wanted to catch the most fish!

Troby was scratching his head, "this has never happened before. Usually you at least snag a few right away..."

Hare had the benefit of not knowing one way or another so he took the simple approach, "maybe I should use a different lure..."

Troby nodded in agreement with an expression indicating he should have thought of it first. He watched as Hare switched lures like he'd been fishing for years. Troby was truly impressed because most folks have trouble at first.

"Okay," said Hare as he got ready for another try, "here we go. Let's do this again!"

Hare was about to cast out his line but stopped abruptly. Troby was about to ask why when Hare walked over to his pack and pulled out the chub of dried meat he brought for lunch. Now Troby *had* to say something...

"What are you doing?"

"I'm going to put a chunk of this meat on the hook," said Hare taking control of the situation, "the fish might smell it and attract them."

"Fish can't smell," said Troby.

"Sure they can," corrected Hare, "most sharks can smell blood hundreds of yards away."

Troby just stood there for a moment, dumbfounded... "how do you know that?"

"Pop happened to mention it one time.... wait a minute!" Hare slowly looked over at Troby and pointed at him smiling, "you're afraid I just might catch the first fish aren't you?!!?

"Harry, you don't put bait on a lure!"

"Look, if I catch the first fish today, I'll say it's because you taught me, okay? Besides, it's worth a try!" With that Hare walked up to the shore and cast out his line as far as he could.

He slowly reeled it all the way back without so much as a bite.

Troby saw it and repeated himself, "I'm tellin' you, you don't put bait on a lure; it's a waste..."

"But look," pointed Hare, "the bait's gone!"

"Of course it is genius because it fell off when you cast out your line," insisted Troby rolling his eyes.

"One more time," said Hare as he broke off another small piece of dried meat and made sure it was firmly on the hook. He counted to three and cast his line even further than before.

The split second the lure hit the water, Hare was violently pulled in. Troby roared out a very loud growl as he sprinted toward the shore. Just then he saw something he would never forget.

At first, Troby saw Hare go flying into the air only to disappear under the water. Just as fast Hare resurfaced as if he was water-skiing. Hare had both hands firmly grasping the fishing pole as whatever he hooked swam erratically but due to Hare's long feet, he was able to remain above water; like body-surfing at Brelojia!

Hare was having a blast, completely void of concern for his life and was laughing and clowning around. He discovered that whatever direction his fishing pole would point, the fish would go in that direction.

Troby just stood absolutely motionless and speechless watching this; no one would ever believe it. Hare was not only water skiing but like the reigns on a horse, he could actually control where his catch went.

Troby started laughing hard when he saw Hare turn the fish toward the shore pulling on the pole to set the hook more making his fish swim faster.....and it was approaching quickly.

Troby stopped laughing and ran for cover..

Hare and whatever he hooked was headed straight for the small beach where they had set up their gear. Troby still couldn't believe what he was watching.

As Hare and his monstrous mystery catch approached the beach, the fish sensed the shallows and put on the brakes by fanning out it's pectoral fins, which were twice the size of Hare. As they hit the small beach, the huge fish now visible, had such enormous pec-fins, many gallons of water were pushed onto the beach bringing other smaller fish with it.

The huge fish stopped dead on the sand but Hare kept going finally letting go of his pole. He flew about ten feet right into the middle of a large mound of green slimy moss. Hare was now covered with smelly, stringy, goo trying to stand while continuing to laugh mainly because he most definitely caught the first fish and several others as well!

Troby quickly walked over to a very slimy Hare and helped free him from his green cocoon. Hare shook the salt water off of him and just stood and stared at the colossal fish he had just landed, literally. It didn't flop as much as the other many smaller fish, but it was gasping for air. To Hare, this was unacceptable.

“We have to get this beast-fish back in the water before it dies,” said Hare with great urgency as he walked tripping over the slime still hanging from him.

Troby was shaking his head from side to side in astonishment... “are you crazy? You want to throw away all that dinner?”

“There's dinner floppin' all over the beach,” said Hare seriously, “besides, this guy is way too big. It'll spoil before you can eat it. I am not going to allow this magnificent fish to die Troby. Let's get that hook out of his mouth and then help me push him back into the water...”

“But,” Troby couldn't believe what he was about to do but decided to side with Hare this time. “Okay. Okay, I'm with you but whatever you do, do not allow those long spines to poke you; they're poisonous and are probably deadly to you. Lets get this done before I change my mind.”

With very careful and considerable effort, Hare's record-making catch not only went down in history, but also went happily back into the water. The other eleven cod and small bass like fish would serve, and be served as a very well earned dinner!

Chapter Nine

Although it was late afternoon, it was dark enough for Hare and Troby to see the flickering fireplace light emanate from within his cave. That could only mean one thing; Hazel-Mae had arrived! Hare started to run toward the cave entrance but Troby stopped him-

"Wait," ordered Troby, "before we left, I saw you put the fire out and there should be an entire den of slinger's guarding Hazel-Mae. So if Hazel didn't light the fire who did? This is not right. You stay here, let me check inside-".

"Yeah, I don't see Brax's ponies either. I'll look outside," said Hare.

"Okay, smell it out first," reminded Troby as he slowly placed all of his gear and burlap sacks of fish he was carrying aside.

Troby stood still, smelling the air. He would walk down a hall waving his arm in the air then stop and smell again. Neither Troby or Hare realized that each of them had highly developed senses of smell and Hare had the added benefit of nearly 360° panoramic vision.

Hare stood in the cave entrance having no news. "I didn't see anything or smell the presence of anyone..."

Troby threw his arms up in frustration, "well, someone lit the fire and-"

"SURPRISE!!!"

From behind Hare, hidden by a bluff and upwind keeping their scent from being detected, was Hazel-Mae, Bop's successor, Rezil and his den of slinger's, and of course Brax's ponies. Blaze and Belle were prancing seeing Hare and Troby hadn't seen Hazel-Mae for years!

Hazel-Mae and Hare instantly ran to each other and embraced with flowing tears. It was a combination of laughter and remorse, elation and tribulation, ultimate joy and gut-twisting regret. Troby got tear-eyed too but of course tried not to show it. The slingers were coiled in their way to show joy as Grashe and Belfg joined them.

"I thought you were gone," said Hazel through still more tears.

Hare hesitated until he could finally say something, “I am so sorry for being such a klutz. I thought I was dead too. But the one who saved me died instead. How am I supposed to live with that?”

“Move on, Harry,” said Hazel-Mae through exhausting emotions, “move on and keep going. Don't allow Bop's death to be in vain. Remember what I told you...”

“No matter,” both Hare and Hazel spoke in unison, “how much it hurts you, never give up.”

They both looked at each other and Hare also looked over at Troby who was caught wiping a tear again. Hare smiled and nodded at Troby because Troby told him the same thing.

Hare was through with tears. He cleared his throat then abruptly excused himself and walked outside to gather his wits then returned with a very determined look on his face.

“Okay,” said Hare clapping his hands together, “I have already promised Troby Bop wouldn't die in vain, and I meant it. So right now, Bop would agree that enough tears have dropped so let's get some fresh seafood cooking and celebrate his life! How does that sound?”

Troby wasted no time setting up a fire-pit with a rotating rotisserie spear so the fish Hare didn't catch but rather shoved onto the shore would cook slowly and evenly. Before everyone knew it, they were enjoying a delicious meal giving everyone much needed sustenance.

Their ceremony for Bop lasted until near sundown when Rezil, Grashe, Belfg, and fellow slingers bid farewell to Hazel, Hare, and Troby. Hare was sad to see them disappear up the gorge wall into the forest and silently wondered if he would ever see his slinger friends again.

Hazel-Mae and Troby stood quietly next to Hare watching him look on well after the snakes vanished into the forest.

“You okay?” asked Troby.

Hare's mind was elsewhere but his response surprised even Hazel...

"...what? Oh, yeah, absolutely. I'm cool man! I'm okay, really! So, let's hit the sack early so we can go fishing tomorrow!"

"Sorry buddy, no can do," said Troby, "time for you to continue your trek. Besides, I'll have seafood for quite a while; it's being dry-cured as we speak! You were right, that beast-fish would have gone to waste."

"And as promised, I may have caught all the fish, but you're the guy who taught me -." Hare stopped in mid sentence... "no can do means you're not going with us."

"You are correct. I was in the middle of something when you guys fell from the clouds into my backyard. Gotta get back to it."

Troby noticed Hare's agitation, "Hey I have things to do. Besides, we're both going in different directions. I gotta say though man, you are the craziest, nut-ball, bunny I've ever met.... actually you're the *only* nut-ball bunny I've ever met but you hang in there."

Hazel-Mae stretched, then yawned which made Hare do the same. Even Troby was tired so they all relaxed in front of the fireplace telling stories and remembering Bop. Eventually, they all fell asleep and woke to a magnificent morning.

Troby helped Hare and Hazel-Mae tighten their saddles and re-packed everything. Troby also gave Hare a special, smaller fishing rig with a reel and a bag of lures. This made Hare do his bunny dance and Troby was happy to get rid of it since he didn't need it and knew Hare could probably use it during his journey.

There was a very emotional goodbye but mostly between Hare and Troby. Hazel-Mae had happy tears streaming down her face as she saw the nine foot plus Troby attempt to hug the three foot plus rabbit! It's not something we see everyday but there was a serious bond between them because despite Troby's extremely unusual entrance into Hare's life, he became a mentor, protector, and trusted friend.

The next chapter in Harrison Hare's musical quest would lead them to their destination; Rhythm Creek. From Troby's cave it was only five miles west to the sea and then north for another three.

Soon, they would be riding Brax's ponies through the peaceful

Twin Canyon Forest then on through the beautiful grassland fields on a perfect day!

As they rode along, Hazel-Mae was amazed that Hare was alive having cheating certain death. She was more amazed since Hare now seemed to not even remember it or at least he didn't care anymore and has moved on. She was becoming more and more impressed at Hare's rapid maturity. Now she fretted over him dealing with a never-ending guilt for Bop's demise. But even that, Hazel noticed, he seemed to be dealing with well. Of course, Hazel didn't see the interaction between Troby and Hare during their 'disagreements' but Troby, being very direct, had set Hare straight and that was a good thing.

They rode for what seemed like a mile and Hare remained silent. Hazel-Mae could tell he was deep in thought since he didn't take out his trumpet and practice like usual. She didn't interrupt him so they simply rode toward their next stop.

Hazel-Mae noticed Hare couldn't stop staring at the inlet as they calmly rode along. Wondering if she was right, she decided to break the silence.

“Hoping to see your big fish?”

Hare chuckled and turned to Hazel, “well sure! I've found that you never know which critters can talk and which ones can't. I was just thinking how interesting it would be to have a conversation with it.”

“What would you say, or ask?”

Hare thought for a second then responded having to clear his throat, “I'd say, 'not long ago I took a life and then not long after that, I gave one back. Glad you're okay'; something like that.”

“You have a big heart Harry,” said Hazel-Mae sincerely.

“Thank you,” responded Hare. “It felt good saving that magnificent fish. It was like redemption in a way, but...”

“But what?” asked Hazel.

“But Bop is still dead and nothing can bring him back,” said Hare reaching into his saddlebag.

Hare pulled out his kick-around, placing the case back into his bag and held the horn to his lips and said, "here's to you Bop!"

They rode along the inlet while Hazel sang scales and Hare harmonized along. Scales were becoming easier for him but it was his lip control he worried about especially with really high notes.

Hazel would council that he might be trying to progress too quickly instead of keeping with the fundamentals first. But, before long the music they made had clouds of butterflies following them while the ponies pranced along!

Finally they were approaching Tidepool Pointe which would mark the final leg of their journey before reaching Rhythm Creek. All the while, Hazel and Hare had been practicing and decided to take a break.

They rode quietly within their own thoughts until Hare saw the breaking waves through the tall reeds and got excited!

"We're at the ocean! I can go body surfing again and catch dinner for us with the cool pole and reel Troby gave me! Can we camp here?!?" asked Hare almost pleading.

Hazel-Mae laughed and said, "sure Harry. I've always loved this little beach. It's a beautiful location. You can expect dazzling sunsets and sunrises I can assure you!"

"I love my home of course but there's so much forest, we don't see full sunsets or sunrises! You can see them if you're at Round Rock Creek but...."

Hare was interrupted by what sounded like faint commotion off in the distance but the sounds were odd. The combined voices sounded like a large group all quarreling after breathing in helium. It was actually funny to Hare but he was more curious than anything. He looked over at Hazel who was obviously attempting to suppress her laughter.

"What is that?" asked Hare chuckling. "I know you know what that is! C'mon, tell the truth!"

“Harry,” responded Hazel-Mae now laughing out loud, “why would you say such a thing? I always tell the truth!”

They turned their ponies toward the new point of interest! Whatever was going on, the closer they got the funnier it became!

Hazel turned to Hare to explain. “Harry my friend, we have arrived at Tidepool Pointe. Tide pools are the top of rock formations that hold water giving tiny sea life their own little community, so to speak. They vary is size and most contain many different species. It's just that in these particular tide pools the many different species within are always arguing!”

“Arguing?” laughed Hare. “What could sea-critters possibly argue about?”

“Good question. Let's find out!”

They approached the first of many large connecting tide pools. Some were stacked on top of each other like floors and others were large and others small. Hazel and Hare dismounted the ponies as Hazel walked them over to the cover of the spruce orchard to give them shade, rest and water. Hare walked over and peered down into the closest pool.

He could see strange and unusual creatures the likes of which he had never seen before. Sure enough, it seemed every resident of these particular tide pools were having a serious dispute... and it was really hard for Hare to keep from howling with laughter hearing these angry, very high pitched voices:

“You're in my area. Stop doing that! I keep telling you, one day you'll get stung and it won't be my fault...”

“You anemones are all the same,” yelled the fiddler crab, “you plant yourselves in one spot and call it yours.”

“You can crawl all over the place but I can't,” countered the anemone, “wanna trade places?”

“I wouldn't trade places with you if you were a stupid starfish,” said the fiddler crab with excessive sarcasm.

The sea urchin sighed, “that made no sense.”

“Don't even listen to that mush head, “snapped the starfish.

“Knock it off already,” yelled the hermit crab, “I absolutely have to crawl to another pool.”

“Then go already. I don't see anyone begging you to stay” said the sea cucumber, “since you *can* crawl, do us all a favor and crawl outa here.”

“Oh yeah? At least I'm not a big fat worm....”, countered the crab.

“That is just cruel and mean,” said the cucumber.

“What do you expect? I'm a crab so I'm crabby okay? Deal with it...”

The tiny flitting sculpin had enough, “hey you dummy crab, crawl outa here and take your attitude with you.”

“Hey, eat me,” yelled the crab.

“No way, how grodie. You wouldn't even make good bait...”

“Whoa, look everybody,” exclaimed the large clump of mussels all in unison. What are youz guys up there lookin' at, eh?”

Silence instantly ensued as all the miniature arguing sea life ceased their verbal volleys of insults and stared up to see two very big faces staring back down. Hare looked up and saw that every level of the tide pools had crazy-looking sea creatures peering over the edge curious as to what was happening in their hood!

Hazel and Hare were smiling as Hazel pointed to each animal in the pools naming them:

“Brittle star, sea anemone, barnacles, fiddler crab, mussels, hermit crab, sea urchin, sculpin, sea cucumber, abalone, bat-starfish, and a friend of yours actually called, a sea-hare!”

“No way, really,” exclaimed Hare?

“This particular species is so named due to its eyes looking like bunny ears, see? It's common name is sea slug...”

“Hey, who are you calling a slug,” snapped the mollusk?

“Oh, I'm so sorry,” apologized Hazel giggling, “let's just stick with sea hare!”

“That's so much better, thank you,” replied the sea hare.

“Hey I'm a hare too,” said Hare.

Hazel stood up,” you get acquainted with your new friends. I'm going to get these guys some new company.”

Hare was curious, “what do you mean?”

“Kelp roots contain lots of tiny sea life that will die being sun baked if we don't relocate them,” explained Hazel-Mae.

“Let me help,” offered Hare as he turned to his tiny new friend,” be right back pal.”

“Okay,” said the sea hare who then raised its funny voice announcing to his neighbors, “we're gonna have company!”

“That's just great,” grumbled the hermit crab, “now there's gonna be all of these new naked crabbies searching for a bigger shell just like I am.”

“At least you have a shell,” said the brittle star-fish, “I can be picked off any time so consider yourself lucky and stop complaining.”

“We get picked off all the time too so shut your plankton hole,” countered the hermit crab.

“Good,” shot back the brittle-star, “I hope you become gull food next...”

Hare turned to follow Hazel-Mae while busting out laughing. Hazel-Mae knew Hare would enjoy the tide pools but what he would see next would amaze him.

“Harry, help me with this please!” asked Hazel. “We need to carry this kelp tree close to the tide pool. Grab it by the root clump.”

“Okay, lets get this over there,” said Hare eager to help.

Hare had no problem pulling the large kelp growth next to the tide pool. He watched while Hazel gently pulled apart the dense root structure disrupting the plethora of tiny, delicate sea life hidden within.

Hare was so mesmerized by what he saw, his face was inches away trying to see the multitude of tiny life that seemed to instantly emerge from every nook and cranny!

“Wow,” exclaimed Hare, “look at those itty-bitty shrimp-like critters! They're so tiny!”

Hazel was laughing, “they're shrimpy shrimp!”

“Look at that crazy thing! It's a centipede or, no, it has fins....what in the world is it?”

“In ancient times...” Hazel gently picked up the nine inch squirming worm, “this guy was called a pile worm or clam worm. Since then it has evolved into part fish with the growth of small pectoral fins which can serve as legs. Notice the small but very pointed dorsal fin...do not touch that-”

“Okay, poisonous I guess?”

“No,” replied Hazel chuckling,” it'll hurt!”

“Yeah, I'll bet! So, if it can swim like a fish, that kinda makes all those legs useless right?”

“Oh no,” answered Hazel as the creature began crawling up her arm, “If you think of all those legs as flippers, this thing can move out! It can also obviously walk and to protect itself, it secretes a mucous type blanket around it which hardens like a force-field.”

“Now, that is cool! Wish I could do that!” said Hare who was wide-eyed and enthralled!

Hazel-Mae gently placed it into the upper tide-pool. “There, that should do.”

“Why did you put it up there?” asked Hare.

“It needs more water since its bigger and longer than these little guys down here. C'mon, help me pick off all these tiny animals before they dry out.”

“Ready-Rabbit, that's me!”

As Hare was helping Hazel transfer all the tiny creatures from the kelp root into the shallow pool, Hare reacted to a tiny minnow being caught in the sea anemone's paralyzing tentacles-

“Hey, look! That little fish is caught by the, which one is that?”

“That's the sea anemone.”

“The fish can't get away, I'll free it!”

“No,” warned Hazel! “don't disturb the natural process. That is how the anemone eats and nourishes itself. You don't want to rob it of it's meal do you?”

Hare paused looking confused, “well, no but aren't we disrupting the natural process by relocating these critters from one place to another?”

Hazel chuckled, “You don't miss much do you? That's a compelling point but millions of these tiny animals trapped in the seaweed trees that break apart and wash up on the beach die everyday! If I can free a few of them, that helps keep their species line going. However, saving that minnow means the anemone will now have to wait until another minnow happens to swim by. It could starve.”

“Well that bites. I wouldn't want someone to take my dinner either!” Hare stared down at the helpless minnow, “sorry Mr. Minnow. Hope you enjoy your lunch Mr. Anemone.”

“Thanks,” answered the anemone, “I'm gonna scarf cuz I'm tired of plankton and floating shards of slime; haven't had a good meal in a week!"

Hazel giggled, "see?!!?"

Hare laughed, "yeah plankton and slime doesn't sound too appetizing to me either, but I understand nature; there is a reason for everything."

"Yes there is precisely! A good example of disrupting nature would be helping something break out of it's eggshell at birth. The intense struggle to free itself and peck, peck, fight, fight through that hard shell is necessary to allow it to gain strength."

"Gotta love it!" exclaimed Hare who was still wide-eyed with curiosity.

He climbed up to see inside the top pool and saw even more unusual creatures that were larger than the bottom pools and also arguing. Hare continued to laugh at the crazy yelling voices but more seriously wondered why. He suddenly jumped down from the upper pool excited! He clapped his hands together and looked at Hazel. "I have a really cool idea!"

Hazel was intrigued, "okay, do tell!"

"If I can teach all of these little critters to sing instead of argue, maybe they would all chill out and become friends!"

"You suddenly got yourself very busy," joked Hazel, "body-surfing, catching dinner, now music lessons?"

"Hey, I have discovered that I can be a very multi-tasking bunny!" Hare started laughing and broke into a quick, rapping bunny dance!

'gonna teach critters to sing,

So they won't be arguing,

They'll be good in their hood,

And cool in their pool'

Hazel was sitting comfortably under a small spruce tree laughing at his antics, “go for it Harry!”

Hare seemed to connect with the sea hare for obvious reasons and asked, “hey Mr. sea-hare, most of you critters can talk so have you all ever tired to sing?”

The sea hare thought for a second then slowly looked up, “what is a sing?”

Hare responded while stammering, “uhm...well, to sing isn't a what, to sing is to make music.”

The sea hare responded, “what is music?”

Hare was silent! He looked dumbfounded over at Hazel-Mae who was still laughing...

“Don't look at me, this is your class! I can't wait to see how this pans out! I think one of your students is waiting for an answer!”

Hare now had to figure out a way to answer the most difficult question he was ever asked. Meanwhile the sea hare was very patiently staring up at Hare waiting for it's difficult question to be answered.

“Okay my little friend, since I can't tell you what music is, I'll have to show you!”

Hare wasted no time walking over to Belle and took out his kick around. Hazel clapped her hands knowing this would be very interesting indeed!

Hare proceeded to play some scales and then broke into a blues riff when Hazel-Mae began to sing along since she knew the melody. Hare didn't see it since he was busy showing off but Hazel did.

Hare's idea worked because as soon as he started playing, the sea anemone released the minnow. It immediately attempted to swim away but the fiddler crab grabbed it. The crab and anemone were always arguing more than the others but when the anemone complained about taking his fish, the crab gave the it back.

"Here you go. Your catch I believe," said the crab.

The anemone hesitated never knowing courtesy from the crab, "yes it is but we can share."

"Thank you," responded the crab as he pinched the minnow in half, "Here's the tail; your favorite right?"

"Yes," said the anemone still shocked at the crabs newly found manners, "Thank you."

"You're welcome and thank you!"

Hazel was amazed since like magic, Hare turned the two worst arguers into friends in seconds!

By now every critter in the upper pools that were able to peer over the edge with their weird eyeballs looked in intense curiosity. The ones in the lower pools were intently looking up with the same anticipation of something....

Hazel-Mae was really laughing now because she knew all too well what a ham Hare was; he was going to milk this opportunity as much as he could! She just sat back against the tree very comfortably watching the show!

Hare stood before his curious audience like an orchestra conductor without a baton.

"Okay everyone, I will now attempt to teach you all how to sing. It is a small part of what we call music. I know you'll enjoy it and maybe one day you will sing instead of argue with each other..."

"But we like to argue," shouted out a crab in the top pool. "It's therapeutic."

"She's right," said the starfish on a rock above the second pool, "we enjoy it."

"It's all we have to do," said the tiny sculpin.

Hare interjected, "well now I'm giving you all something different to do that will make your lives much happier!"

The anemone in the bottom pool agreed, "He's right, isn't he crabby?"

"Yes, that right," the former nasty crab said, "as soon as we heard the sound, we were friends! I say we go for it!"

"Yeah, c'mon everyone," shouted the anemone so everyone could hear it, "let's try something new and different okay?!!?"

There was a silence as if waiting for a verdict. Then the inaudible chatter ensued, when finally everyone cheered in agreement!

Hazel-Mae stood up from her comfortable place under the spruce tree clapping and laughing! She walked across the beach to join Hare in his first gig as a music teacher!

"Okay," began Hare pointing to each pool, "usually from bottom to top, it goes baritone, tenor, alto, then soprano. Baritone is the low voice then tenor is the-"

Hazel-Mae nudged him whispering, "keep it simple maestro! Besides, you will not find a tenor or baritone here I can promise you!"

Hare started cracking up at his obvious oversight. When he composed himself and looked up, he surveyed all the confused expressions and staring eyeballs focused on him and he started his doubled-over-laugh-attack again. Finally, he tried to get serious!

"Okay, okay, sorry. Let's have some fun and play a game. Everybody likes games right?!"

"What is a game?" asked the anemone.

Hare looked at Hazel without expression and whispered, "tough crowd, man."

Hazel now had a laugh-attack herself at Hare's deadpan response, "you're into it now maestro! I'm just a spectator...!"

Hare turned back to his confused audience. "okay friends, let's start over. We're going to have some fun and if you all have fun with it too, your arguing days will be over! Ready? Hare raised his trumpet to his lips and played a few warm-up notes then began the lesson.

The next day, Hazel and Hare were enjoying a peaceful, calm lunch recalling their tidepool encounter.

"…..I think it's amazing that you actually taught tide-pool creatures how to sing," said Hazel taking a bite of sprout bread, "that's one for the record books!"

"It's definitely some kinda record because I don't sing," chuckled Hare as he wiped his mouth with a towel placing it down. Hazel had been watching him as she took a drink of tea.

"What's wrong Harry? Something's bothering you."

"Naw, I'm okay. It's just that I'll never forget this journey you set up for me and it certainly isn't over yet. I was just thinking about all the new friends I've met and the one's I have yet to meet. It's beyond exciting but when I finally get back home, I live so far away it'll make it tough to visit everyone out this way again."

"Yes, that's true but think about what will happen once you do get home. There will be a celebration like no other. Many of your friends are missing you as we speak."

"Ha! You sure about that? Last time they saw me I was just an immature, blubbering baby."

"I believe your original assessment was a 'big fat whining bunny-butt'!

Hare busted up, "yeah, that too! You remember everything don't you?"

"I remembered it because it was funny! And, hear me bunny-butt, you have come a long way in a short time. Just four days ago your were indeed a whining bunny but since then you have fended off a wolf pack, have no problem camping out in the elements, surf on the back of gigantic fish, and as if that weren't enough, cheated certain death. Sure, you're reckless sometimes but with everything you've been through I think you're dealing with it just fine, and that includes what happened to Bop. Yes, I'd say you've changed... changed for the better. And that, deserves a surprise!"

"A surprise? What have you dreamed up this time?"

"When was the last time you were on a boat?"

Chapter Ten

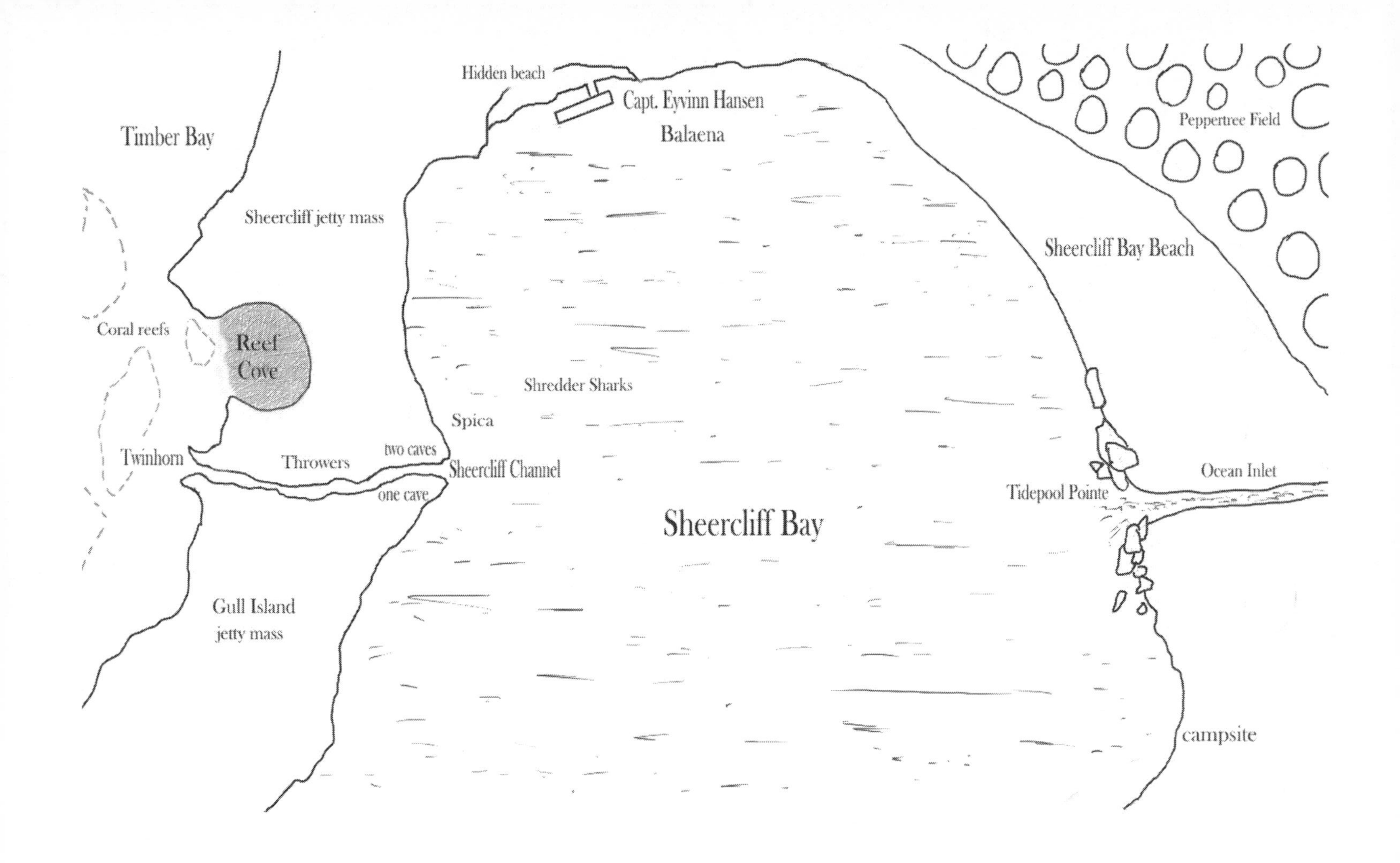
Hidden beach
Capt. Eyvinn Hansen
Balaena
Peppertree Field
Timber Bay
Sheercliff jetty mass
Sheercliff Bay Beach
Coral reefs
Reef Cove
Shredder Sharks
Spica
two caves
Twinhorn
Throwers
Sheercliff Channel
Ocean Inlet
Tidepool Pointe
one cave
Sheercliff Bay
Gull Island jetty mass
campsite

Hare shot up from his seat nearly spilling his food on the ground, “really? Are you kidding?!!? No... you wouldn't joke about that. Oh man, how awesome, I can't wait! When? What kind of boat?”

“Well, first of all, so you're aware, going by boat is necessary this time to get through the twin jetty's over there,” said Hazel pointing toward the sheer cliffs. “That huge split you see is the Sheercliff Channel. We will be going through that since the jetty rock formation is impassable for us over land.”

“What's on the other side?” asked Hare excited.

“Our destination Harry,” Hazel-Mae said smiling! “Rhythm Creek is just on the other side of the twin jetty's!”

A very excited Hare and Hazel spent the day relaxing and playing around with their newly found friends at Tidepool Pointe. They made a comfortable camp close to the tide pools which gave Hare a chance to practice and show off for his students!

Following a beautiful day and an equally gorgeous afternoon, Hare sat on a log polishing his trumpets while Hazel had been relaxing sitting in her bedroll reading by the campfire. Suddenly, she got up and walked out to the breakwater.

“Where are you going?” asked Hare.

“I'll be right over here,” answered Hazel, “arranging our transportation.”

She stood with her toes in the sand while the foaming fringes of the spent waves washed around her feet. She didn't make a sound or even move but just stared up into the indigo sky. Hare watched her thinking she was going to speak bird or some ancient dialect that would summon fish or something but he was mistaken. She just stood there when suddenly she shrieked so loud Hare covered his ears.....

“E Y V I N N H A N S E N– A H O Y Y Y Y Y !!!”

With that Hazel-Mae walked back to their camp site without saying anything. She calmly sat back down on her bed roll and resumed studying her updated dossiers of the area. She knew Hare was dying to start asking questions so she calmed his curiosity.

"You asked before, when and what kind of boat? When we sail will be at first light tomorrow. As to what kind of boat? I don't even know that since it's been a long time since I've sailed with him, but that will be up to our host, or in this case, our Captain."

"... Captain? A real Captain?!!?" asked Hare excitedly.

Hazel hesitated, "... well he owns the ship. In most nautical arenas if you own the vessel, it makes you a Captain, or as many like to be called, 'Skipper'."

"Really?" asked Hare surprised. "I thought there was more to it than that."

"There is much more to it than just owning the vessel as you'll see tomorrow. Being a sea Captain, or Skipper, means you have to know how to navigate a huge floating vessel in a possibly very angry ocean with obstructions you can't see that could turn even a large ship into driftwood. Plus you have a crew relying on you with their lives and that's just the tip of a very large iceberg. Trust me Harry, there is nothing easy about it. That's why it's so rewarding when you master it. Of course that's true about any goal in life."

"Betcha I could do it! I'd be the greatest Captain on the high seas and I'd-"

B O O O O O M

Hare flew out of his skin being startled more than ever by the explosion. It was so sudden he lost his balance and fell down...

"Whoa! What was that?"

Hazel was doubled over laughing having shown her practical-joker side! "That, Captain Harry is a signal cannon!"

"Oh sure laugh it up! Why did you conveniently forget to tell me that was going to happen?!"

"I'm sorry," Hazel tried to speak through her laughter, "I just wanted to get your attention-!"

"Hey now," said Hare who was laughing too," I never did anything to deserve that, so I owe you one!"

"Oh man," said Hazel-Mae wiping laughter tears away, "yes you do Harry, yes you do, but that was so good!"

"Yeah, you'll get yours," said Hare laughing even more now, "I'm assuming that was an answer from our Captain, or Skipper?"

Hazel's laughter subsided a little, "Arrr matey, that be correct. Skipper Eyvinn is always early so we better be too otherwise we'll hear about it."

"So, what's the deal with this captain guy? You make it sound as if he's an angry grump."

Hazel-Mae got serious."Captain Eyvinn Hansen is what is called an 'old salt'. He's been operating a transport and charter service for as long as I've been assigned to this territory. He's seen it all including the deaths of his two sons, taken years ago just three weeks apart but-"

"-that is so sad," interrupted Hare.

"-yes, it was. But you need to know that Captain Eyvinn isn't completely human. He's a Lemuriped, half human and half ring-tail Lemur. To you he will look very odd with the huge eyes that don't blink and mouse-like features, but do not underestimate him, and don't stare at him. He's the best boating pilot anywhere. And, like us all, if you treat him with the respect he is due, he will treat you the same. However, the reverse is also true."

"Hey, if you say this guy is cool, that's good enough for me."

"Just remember what he says, goes. If you're not sure about something, ask. He's very competent and strict on safety as he should be but he'll have a crew that will help you also. Just be yourself! You were obviously raised with good manners toward others and you're not afraid to get involved. If he asks you for help simply say, Aye-aye Captain!"

"I, I Captain?" asked Hare.

“Aye-aye Harry, that's perfect!” said Hazel, “we better turn in. Make sure to get plenty of rest. From sunrise until around noon the seas should be relatively calm but the tides always get choppy later in the afternoon. Oh and, you're in for quite an adventure because this will not be a pleasure cruise.”

“Understood.”

The brisk morning ocean air found Hare yawning as his eyes opened. He wasted no time getting out of his bedroll and ready for the next adventure! Finally, after all of the dreams he's had about sea travel, it was going to happen!

It was still dark but the bright moon made it easy for Hare to quietly roll up his bed and get things packed in his saddle bag. He didn't want to wake up Hazel or disappoint Captain Eyvinn before even meeting him by being late.

Just then Hazel began rustling and stretching in her bedroll as Hare was standing at the waters edge straining to hear something. She got up and gathered her things packing them in her saddlebag.

“Good Morning,” said Hazel as she fed the ponies some oats.

“Good morning to you,” replied Hare, “and what a fine morning it is! I hope Captain Eyvinn has a place for Brax's ponies.”

“Oh yes, he's well aware. Like I said, he's a transport skipper and has hauled more animals of various types than I could name! Blaze and Belle will be very comfortable I can assure you!”

“That's good,” said Hare, “I'm becoming pretty attached to them!”

“Hard not to,” replied Hazel!

“Hey, will Captain, or, uh, Skipper....”

“He likes 'Skipper'.”

“-will Skipper Eyvinn be firing off that cannon again?”

“I doubt it,” replied Hazel flatly, “why, do you want him to?”

“I was actually thinking about firing it off myself!”

Hazel got serious again, “now Harry, its only used when needed. If he needs to fire it off again perhaps he'll let you but remember a signal cannon is not a toy.”

“Understood,” replied Hare as he stood at the breakwater tapping his long foot nervously in anticipation.

Finally, the dawn began to break with the first hue of daylight. Hare heard the sound of someone singing off in the distance and instantly initiated a serious bunny dance!

“There he is!!! He's coming! Yay! Oh man, this is so awesome!”

Hazel shook her head up and down, “Yep, right on time as usual!”

Hare stopped jumping around seeing the ship approach. Through the fog he saw a dim, flickering light illuminating the water ahead and a red and green smaller light on each side.

The distant, slightly raspy though articulate singing voice could be clearly heard-

I come from a long-long line o' smelly skippers,

From sloops, ketches, and rotted clippers,

I've 'et barnacle stew and drank shark-blood tea,

That's why its the only life for me,

I want salt in my face and the wind at my back,

To hear the brass bell toll and the canvas crack,

Taking me to another distant shore,

Where I can sail on and find a thousand more......

Hare was about to go crazy with anticipation. He remembered the pictures his father would show him of the beautiful three masted galleons and other tall ships. He envisioned one of those majestic vessels with the ornate woodworking, the many small cannon doors and all the sails and rigging. It was still dark but what finally came into view wasn't what Hare expected!

Hare whispered, "looks like it already sank."

"Shhh," commanded Hazel quietly! "Never forget how fast sound can travel over water. Listen Harry, if Skipper Eyvinn trusts it, so do I."

"Okay, that's good enough for me. Sorry, I meant no disrespect."

"It may not be pretty to look at but then it's still dark. Soon you'll be sailing on the 'Balaena'. That means 'Sea Monster' in Latin and is a very apropos name. Trust me, if Skipper Eyvinn built it, you can count on it."

Hare's mouth dropped open as he slowly looked over at Hazel-Mae, "His boat is hand made?"

"Every nautical inch."

"Now that is amazing. He must really know his stuff!"

"Again, you can count on it."

Skipper Eyvinn's vessel was under oar power since they weren't yet under way. The boat slowed and stopped roughly 50 yards from the beach as Hare saw two of Eyvinn's crew row a skiff toward shore.

Hazel turned to Hare, "when they get close to shore, you'll be thrown a rope. Grab it and help pull them in. I'll get the ponies ready."

"Aye-aye Skipper!" said Hare practicing.

Hare did as instructed and before he knew it, the skiff was pulled onto the beach as the two crew members of the Balaena jumped out.

"Hello," said Hare as he got his first look at Eyvinn's kind. He didn't stare because he didn't care. He was ready for this and wanted the crew to know it.

“Hello there! My name is Llars and my mate here is Peder,” said Llars extending his hand.

Hare shook his hand firmly looking right into his eyes as his father had taught him, “I am Harrison Hare and you most likely know Hazel-Mae.”

Both Llars and Peder bowed as they had only heard the stories. Peder, spoke, “we know only of you my lady, but it is our privilege to finally meet the legend.”

“Please guys,” said Hazel sincerely, “thanks for that but every one of us are legends. Nice to meet you. I know we have to get going so here are the ponies.”

“We will get them into the skiff right away,” said Llars.

“Can I help?” asked Hare.

“Sure,” said Llars as he picked up a long board from the bottom of the skiff, “this is a ramp for the ponies. Just place it right there if you would please.”

Hare placed the ramp on the skiff's edge and looked up to Llars, “is here good?”

“Perfect,” said Llars.

They escorted the ponies into the skiff and when all was ship-shape, they rowed off toward the Balaena.

Hare was excited beyond belief! He was fidgeting which Hazel noticed when he suddenly blurted out a request!

“Hey once we get going, is there anything I can do like batten down the hatches or man the bilge? Anything like that?”

“Wish you could,” replied Peder chuckling at Hare's valiant attempt at 'sailor-talk'. “It would be a great comfort to have another hand on board but the Skipper is very serious about safety. Once under way, he might allow you to help but if you don't know what you're doing, there are a thousand ways to get seriously hurt or worse."

Hare stammered, "well unfortunately, I have no sailing experience."

Llars patted Hare's shoulder and smiled, "You don't need any. We won't be sailing for a while if at all. There's rarely wind on this side of the jetty due to the Sheercliff Peaks mountain range. We'll be under power until we reach the channel but once we get to the other side and clear the reefs, hopefully we'll have sufficient wind to raise our sails and enjoy the pleasures of sailing but that's questionable."

"What do you mean, under power?" asked Hare.

"You'll be briefed once on board. We'll see about you joining the crew in some capacity but I can't promise anything as all decisions fall on the Skipper. Right now though, please have a seat until we arrive at the Balaena."

"Aye-aye!" said Hare feeling like a real sea-faring bunny now.

As they approached Skipper Eyvinn's vessel, Hare saw him peer over the railing and noticed right away that the Skipper looked straight at him. At first Hare was nervous but without thinking, he blurted out, "Ahoy Skipper! Harrison Hare at your service, sir!"

The Skipper ignored Hare but welcomed Hazel-Mae vocally while his glare... was still on Hare. Meanwhile the ramp was fitted, the ponies were unloaded and the skiff was winched up and secured. Before long they were all on board.

Skipper Eyvinn approached Hazel-Mae and bowed. Hazel-Mae took his hands in hers.

"It is such a joy to see you again Skipper!"

"My dear Hazel-Mae, you disappeared so quickly last time, I didn't get an opportunity to thank you for the repair work. Your Brelojia shipwrights saved my butt."

Hare started snickering. The skipper slowly turned to face him without expression. Hare stopped snickering.

Hazel smiled pointing at Hare, “this is my courageous companion, Harrison Hare. Harry, meet Skipper Eyvinn Hansen.”

Once again, Hare stared him straight in the eye and extended his hand. The Skipper demonstrated just how strong a mariners grip can be. Hare didn't flinch but shook the Skippers gnarled hand strongly.

“Welcome aboard seaman Harry. Safety first, never doubt me, and never jump overboard for a swim. My word is law once we're under way and if ye gotta spew chunks, it better be overboard. Mr. Llars will fill you in when needed and Mr. Peder will see to your quarters. Gentlemen, please take Seaman Harry down below for a float and acclimation. We shove off in half an hour.”

Llars and Peder were already standing by to escort Hare below, and just as they were to answer orders, Hare was ready. All three of them responded at the same time, “Aye-aye Skipper!”

Hare smiled broadly as he saw a slight smile come over the Skipper. They walked toward the doorway that would lead them into the belly of the vessel.

“What's a float?” asked Hare.

“Most call it a life preserver. It'll keep you afloat if the ship sinks.”

“Okay, but this boat is pretty solid. I doubt it could sink,” said Hare stamping his long right foot onto the deck.

Llars instantly responded, “shhh, quiet my land-lubber friend! Don't e v e r let the Skipper hear you call the Balaena a boat. You'll be swimming home! Just know that every ship can sink. That's why we are students of the sea and follow orders. C'mon, time to get below. We'll be under way in thirty.”

Hare followed Llars and Peder through a doorway and down some steps. Meanwhile Hazel turned to Skipper Eyvinn.

“Sorry about vanishing after you docked at Dolphin Cove. I had urgent business.”

"My dear, no explanations are necessary I assure you," responded the Skipper, handing her a float, "your people not only repaired my damaged keel but found a significant amount of other little problems I was not aware of. I am actually in your debt. Thank you."

"I'm very happy about that. Our people take great pride in their work."

"So I've been telling everyone I know!"

"Thank you Skip, much appreciated!"

Hazel took a moment to look around since it had been many years since she did any business with the Skipper and in fact hadn't been out to sea since. She finally looked over at Skipper Eyvinn with astonishment.

"Captain Eyvinn Hansen, what did you do? Your ship looks so different, what is this huge machine here where your poop deck used to be?"

"Got rid of the poop," chuckled the Skipper, "remember when you were on board last and we were heading toward Val-Eschutre?"

"How could I forget?" laughed Hazel. "Halfway into our return to the mainland the wind died and so did our trip!"

"Precisely. Well, this contraption right here eliminates the wind altogether. This is my own special steam engine, custom made for the Balaena!"

"Steam," said Hazel nodding," yes, ingenious idea! Very impressive!"

"Well, impressive or not I got tired of losing business due to Mother Nature's undesirable sense of humor. Besides, to be honest, I've truly, deep down never enjoyed sailing.... and that, is between just you and me!"

"I've always known Skip," said Hazel-Mae.

"You have," asked the Skipper? "It was that obvious? I thought I was concealing my displeasure with great success all these years!"

“Um, well it was your language when you thought no one could hear you,” Hazel-Mae said smiling.

“Yes, of course. Apologies my lady but I am a sailor! Well, used to be,” said the Skipper laughing and pointing around, “if you notice I scaled down the sailing operation and now just have a mainsail and jib with a stowed spinnaker. Got rid of most of the huge jungle of rigging too.”

“So I see,” replied Hazel looking around smiling, “you've been busy! This refitting must have taken a long time and cost you a few shiny pennies!”

“Oh yes, a few pennies indeed but all of those canvas sails were more expensive to have repaired or replaced than all of Balaena's brass fittings combined. The expense went on and on...darn near broke me! So I'm back to basics with sailing and utilize it when necessary. Besides, I'm old! Playing the swashbuckling sea captain is a game for the young!”

“So is someone contemplating retirement,” asked Hazel?

Skipper Eyvinn laughed out loud, “bite thy tongue! Never! Banish the thought!”

Hazel laughed, “I thought so! Show me your steam engine!”

Hazel was excited always having been impressed with Skipper Eyvinn's creative work and his brilliant engineering mind. He held her arm as they walked from the bridge up a small flight of steps onto where a small observation deck used to sit at the ships stern, usually called a 'poop deck'. Skipper Eyvinn continued the tour...

“...this custom engine is a compact design providing more than enough propulsion to buzz all over this bay and beyond. No more being at the winds mercy! It's several decks above the prop shafts so all linkage is streamlined. I had your people fabricate extra large props out of thick bamboo so the props are lightweight, easy to replace, won't rust, inexpensive, mostly impervious to boring worms and other nasties, and at full steam I can reach roughly twelve knots. Plus it's designed to be as quite as possible and the best part is all I have to do is steer! You'll see once we get under way.”

"I am very, very impressed Skipper," said Hazel looking around smiling.

"I can't demonstrate it now but if you notice the entire engine assembly is not fixed to the deck. It takes a few minutes to disconnect various components but the whole engine apparatus is designed to be lowered into a hold beneath the deck allowing us to have a clear deck when the steam power isn't needed. I'm still working on it actually. Darn near had to rebuild the whole ship to do all this but the hassles and bad language was worth it!"

"I love it", responded Hazel shaking her head side to side, "you always were amazingly inventive. My favorite was the Dolphin Cove pier you helped design and built at Pristine Bay. For decades that project was on the table but nothing was ever done. Once you found out about it, the whole thing was completed in less than a year!"

"Yes, that was a fun project, and challenging but your people are amazingly gifted so don't exclude yourself! I learned a lot from your talented clan. Many of those lessons I utilized rebuilding the old shipyard."

Hazel excitedly jumped up and down, "Oh yes, I heard the reports! You transformed the yard you learned at into a new and modern operation! I'm so proud of you Skipper! You have been busy!"

"Yes ma'am, Kristal Harbor is doing very well. Now then, back to business. Tell me, in your opinion can your furry friend competently execute light duty aboard this vessel?"

"Well, that all depends on what light-duty entails of course," replied Hazel, "but he's never been on the ocean much less any sea-going vessel. I can guarantee you of one thing, he's fearless and will put everything he has into whatever is asked of him."

"Is he rambunctious, reckless, you know, acts before he thinks?"

"Yes," answered Hazel honestly, "he has demonstrated that occasionally but he's young. And, like us all, we learn by doing. Trust me Skipper, he will surprise you! But, why not ask him directly?"

"That won't be necessary," answered the Skipper smiling. "How's his balance?"

Hazel-Mae giggled.... "with those big long feet? His balance is great and he won't slip in sea water. He'd also make a great lookout too since he has full 360 degree vision. Yes sir, he's good to go Skip!"

"360 vision you say? That's great but there are some with crystal clear 20/20 that remain blind. But, if you believe in him that much, I will also," said the Skipper who took a deep breath, "ALL HANDS ON DECK! TIME TO GET UNDER WAY. Seaman Hazel here we go! Please don your float and we'll head out."

"Aye, aye Skipper!" Hazel complied instantly.

Llars, Peder, and Hare appeared on deck. Llars responded first-

"Present on deck Skipper."

"Present on deck Skipper," responded Peder.

"PRESENT ON DECK SKIPPER," yelled Hare!

Both Hazel and the Skipper smiled because Hare didn't have to yell but that showed the Skipper Hare was ready as were his crew. Hazel knew the Skipper liked Hare as everyone who ever met him did but of course he chose not to show it.

"Mr. Llars, fly all colors then light 'er up. Mr. Peder, have Seaman Harry assist you in stowing lanterns and drawing in the oars then prepare him for push-pole duty."

"Aye-aye Skipper," responded Peder and Llars instantly.

Hare was clapping his hands and smiling from long ear to long ear! He was hoping the Skipper would find something for him to do instead of having him sit out the voyage down below.

Peder knew he was anxious to help out so he approached Hare smiling, patting him on the back, "welcome to the crew of the Balaena! Follow me and be careful where you place those big feet!"

The sun was rising fast casting warm sunlight on their

surroundings and also their destination. Llars raised their colors then proceeded to get the steam engine going.

Hazel-Mae joined the Skipper on the fly-bridge watching as Peder taught Hare his very first task as an actual crew member on an actual ship!

She knew Hare was going to exceed everyone's expectations... exactly how he would achieve that, no one could have ever imagined or believed.

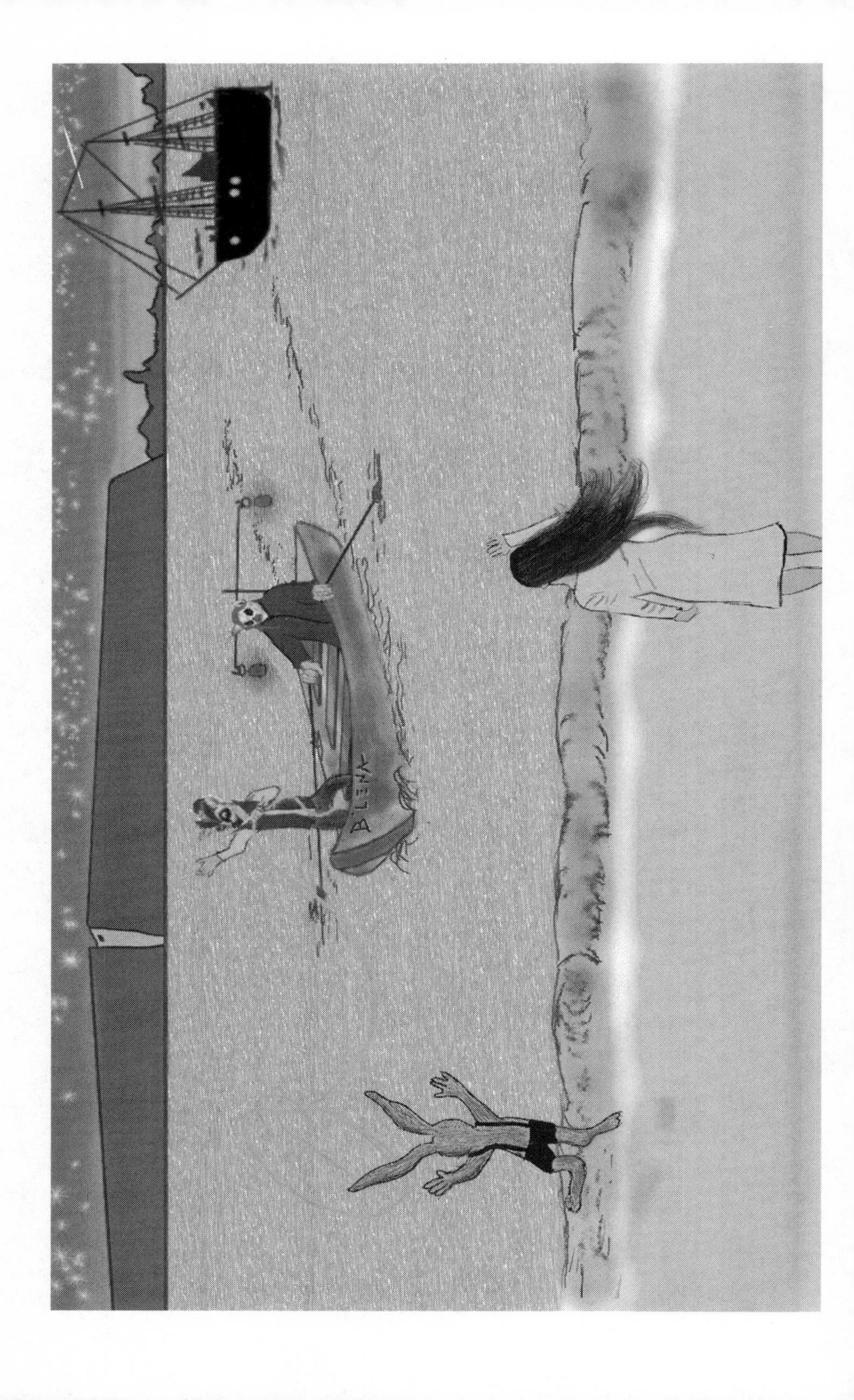

Chapter Eleven

"Full steam ahead at your order Skipper," announced Llars.

"Very well Mister Llars, let the Balaena fly!"

"Aye-aye Skipper," smiled Llars as he sounded the ships brass bell at his station three times indicating 'going full-steam, hang on to something'.

The Skipper would then duplicate the order verbally, "FULL STEAM AHEAD, STAND ALERT ALL HANDS."

Peder had shown Hare how to hold and effectively use the long push-pole that would be used to help fend off the ship if it drifted too close to the narrow walls of the channel. Although the channel was several hundred yards away, it wouldn't take long for them to reach it.

"Okay Seaman Harry," instructed Peder, "the full steam ahead order has been called so ready yourself because we're going to be moving out quickly."

"Aye-aye sir," answered Seabunny Harry who was beyond thrilled! He remained focused on his task at hand especially when the ship propelled forward with a jolt.

"Skipper Eyvinn," exclaimed Hazel, "I never dreamed a ship could actually go this fast!"

"Oh, we're not at full steam yet," laughed the Skipper, "she's just gettin' warmed up!"

"How did you acquire such tremendous speed from a home-made steam engine?"

"Take a guess! You have a regular size engine with a boiler twice the size with streamlined linkage and an extra wide prop..."

Hazel smiled having been challenged by the Skipper to guess! She thought about it, looked at him then down at Llars keeping the fire going, then back at him. Her eyes finally widened as she slowly voiced her guess... "Captain Eyvinn...you're using Val-Eschoute coal aren't you?!!?"

"Affirmative!" answered the Skipper smiling.

"Eyvinn, that is seriously expensive and very hard to mine," Hazel said watching Llars shovel the dark purple substance into the cauldron hopper as it flared brightly.

"Yes it is my dear but well worth it and a lot less costly than a ton of canvas sails and a competent crew to trim them! A lightweight vessel and engine power is the future. Long travel on the open sea is still reserved for the tall ships but for what I do, this is it!"

Just then full speed was established as the ship gradually but gently increased in speed to the point where Hare's long ears were blown back! Just as quickly the Balaena settled into a smooth and enjoyably quick ride over flat, calm waters.

The sun was now casting breathtaking ribbons of color across the sky as the day was warming. Hare watched dumbfounded as the eighty foot high jetty mountains seemed to grow taller right before his eyes.

Hazel looked at Hare on the deck below calmly talking to Peder as if he had been doing this his whole life! She knew Hare wasn't afraid and she knew the Skipper sensed it too. However, the Skipper kept an eye on him anyway since everything that occurred aboard his vessel was his responsibility, especially the crew.

Hazel-Mae stood on the fly-bridge with her long, waterfall of silk black hair flowing and dancing in the wind. The last time she sailed with Skipper Eyvinn, they actually *were* sailing. She took a deep breath and smiled taking in the wonderfully invigorating sea air!

The Balaena elegantly sliced her way through the calm bay as if skating on ice. The narrow opening to the channel was now becoming more visible giving the Skipper concern...

"I was afraid of that," Skipper said to Hazel-Mae pointing at the channel, "if you remember the last time we sailed together the channel was much wider..."

"Yes," replied Hazel pointing toward the sky, "look up there at two caves... both openings are nearly next to each other now. I'd give it less than a year and the channel will close altogether even for skiffs."

Hazel looked over at the Skipper who looked at her, "can you make it through there? Can you thread the needle?"

"Probably, but that would constitute an assumption and I never assume," replied the Skipper not sounding very reassuring, "I'm bettin' our port and starboard oars are too long and our draft is in question. No telling what the underwater topography looks like now days and I will not risk ripping the Balaena in half – we'd be shredder shark fodder in no time."

"Yes, "agreed Hazel, "it looks questionable. I'm with you Captain."

"MR. LIARS, FULL STOP PLEASE AND LOWER SKIFF. AMIDSHIPS DROP ANCHOR, EXPECT FIFTY FEET THEN REPORT TO THE STERN PLATFORM."

"Aye-aye Skipper", replied all stations.

"Let's go have a look shall we?" asked the Skipper.

"Yes Captain, we shall indeed!" answered Hazel enthusiastically.

As the Skipper turned to secure the bridge, Hazel smiled broadly as she watched Peder show Hare how to drop anchor and tie off the line. Hare's intense concentration made Hazel-Mae proud he was doing so well!

Llars lowered the skiff onto the water then swung the ramp over for everyone to walk down.

"Let's go everyone," ordered the Skipper. "First Mate Llars will stay behind to stand watch while we go and see if we can even get through."

After Peder and Hare dropped anchor and secured their station, they were walking toward the skiff platform when Hare thought he saw something. Peder kept walking but Hare had stopped staring out at the water.

Peder stopped and reminded Seaman Harry, "what are you doing? Time to disembark! We have to check the channel-"

Seaman Harry cut him off, yelling, "that's my fish!!! My beast-fish... I saved him from-!!!" Hare was now jumping up and down doing his bunny-dance pointing out toward the channel. He then ran toward the bow of the ship while everyone else was watching him go from able seaman to screaming lunatic...

"....he's going to jump," said Peder, "NO HARRY DON'T.... he's going to jump-"

"BLAST," roared the Skipper, "he sure is! Hurry, Peder into the skiff! Hazel, I must insist that you remain on board not only to insure your safety but to assist Mr. Llars. We have to get him out! It's morning and the nasties are hungry."

Llars hurried from the stern platform up toward the bow when he saw Hare about to jump from the bowsprit.... "No, don't jump! There are-"

Just then Llars saw, as everyone else did too, Hare disappearing over the bow which was followed by the splash.

"MAN OVERBOARD SKIPPER!" yelled Llars pulling a small telescope from it's holster. "CHECKING 360 WITH THE GLASS."

"Thank you Mr. Llars," answered the calm Skipper about to speak again, "Mr. Peder..."

"SHARKS SIGHTED SKIPPER! yelled Llars," ONE O'CLOCK, PORT SIDE BOW!"

Hazel screamed as she could now see Hare trying to swim without the help of moving waves and there were five predator shredder sharks headed straight for him.

The Skipper and Peder were already in motion but the Skipper stopped short with enough time to get back to the ship...

"MR. LlARS, HARPOON ON THE DOUBLE!"

"I got it," said Hazel as she not only knew where it was but was right next to it. She handed it carefully but briskly to the Skipper.

"Thank you," said the Skipper looking at her remaining

confidently calm.

The skiff was rowed as fast as Peder could row. They moved quickly but were up against five shredder sharks that strike at anything hungry or not.

One harpoon and a skiff against five would be no match.

Hazel once again watched helplessly as Hare was caught in yet another 'sure-death' situation. She nearly broke down again sensing the terrible feeling of hopelessness that she felt watching Hare fall into the chasm of Snake Gorge. Now she was watching in horror as the sharks closed in....

Llars cupped his hands over his mouth yelling, "SKIPPER, THERE'S SOMETHING OUT THERE. IT'S REALLY BIG AND MOVING FAST TOWARD YOU. PULL BACK!"

Hazel got up wiping away tears and ran to the aft deck railing. As she quickly brushed her hair out of her face, she saw a massive mound of water moving very quickly toward the sharks who were now in an attack pattern around the helpless, flailing Hare.

No sooner did the massive mound of moving water pass Hare, it then displayed it's ominous and threatening spine-filled dorsal fin and massive pectoral fins as this monster was now visible. When the gigantic fish finally rose it's head above the water and opened it's cavernous mouth with long, sword like teeth, suddenly the sharks were no where to be seen. The huge fish snapped it's mouth closed sending waves of water in all directions.

Meanwhile, Hazel-Mae, the Skipper, Peder, and Llars could only look on in astonishment as the whale-fish lowered all of it's intimidating spine-filled fins and swam straight toward the still flailing Hare. He stayed afloat due to his life preserver but was exhausted and watched as 'his' fish got closer.

The beast-fish got right next to him and fanned out a smooth fin void of spines and then eliminated Hare's curiosity of whether it could talk or not.

"Climb on! You're safe my friend!"

Hare struggled to climb onto the large fin. He sat trying to catch his breath and finally replied while patting his fish like a pet...

"Thank you, thank you, thank you, I don't know what I would've done."

"You saved my life, and I returned the favor," said the giant fish, "my honor is secure and you are alive so I do believe that makes us even!"

Hare was still breathing heavy, "I took a life recently and not long after....I gave one back. I am SO glad you're okay. And yes, we most certainly are even!"

Meanwhile the Skipper and Peder continued to row toward Hare who was resting on the fish's giant fin appearing to be having a pleasant chat with the creature as if it was an everyday event. Despite Hare's failure to follow orders, the Skipper discovered a new respect for Hare because he thought he had seen it all.

As the skiff got closer to Hare and the fish, the Skipper and Peder could hear the ensuing conversation...

Fish: "... in that case, you will need a guide to weave you through the narrow channel-"

The skiff pulled up next to the massive fish and stopped... both Peder and Skipper Eyvinn remained speechless. Finally, the Skipper concurred...

"We were about to check that..."

"So, that's your ship?" asked the fish.00 "I recognize the hull. I've seen you around for quite a while. And, if you are friends with my little life-saver here, you are friends to me. So, you guys must be in a hurry to want to risk the channel. Why not go through the Gull Jetty pass?"

"We're headed to Cedar Forest, docking at Briar pier," answered Skipper Eyvinn.

Hare's huge fish didn't respond immediately but remained still, thinking, then asked the Skipper....

“I couldn't tell if you have a removable keel...do you?”

“Of course,” replied Skipper Eyvinn, “have to on these waters.”

“Right, okay, how about this,” said the fish, “to fully pay my life-debt, remove your keel then rig up a bit to fit across my mouth and I will escort you through Sheercliff Channel to Reef Cove. I cruise these waters all the time and can further guide you safely around the reefs up until Briar pier if needed... after that you are on your own and my debt is paid. Agreed?”

“You have no debts with me but, agreed,” answered the Skipper.

Hare spoke up, “wait! Your debt was already paid by saving me from those sharks. But, uhm, if you insist on being our escort we will not argue the point!”

“Let's get going then!” exclaimed the fish.

“Very much appreciated,” said the Skipper. “What be your name friend?”

“Well,” chuckled the fish, “I have many names most of which I won't repeat but in my home waters I'm known as Spica.”

“... that be Latin for Spike,” the said Skipper.

Spica bobbed his head up and down, “you are correct Captain! You speak it do you sir?”

“My ship is named the Balaena,” answered the Skipper. Not many have heard a big fish laugh but Spica instantly responded...

“Sea monster,” chuckled Spica, “and all of this time I thought the balaena was me!”

The Skipper howled with laughter, slapping his hand down on the skiff, ”well Spica, now I have no choice but to share that name with you. Let's get you back to the ship and figure out a comfortable way to turn you into a water-horse!”

Hazel-Mae and Llars were now both standing together near where the skiff would dock at the ships stern platform. As the huge beast-fish and skiff got closer to the Balaena, Llars took the line and pulled the skiff in for docking.

Hazel was beside herself being amazed once again shaking her head from side to side. She was in awe of the indescribable way Hare could somehow always seem to squeeze his way out of very serious situations while remaining calm as if nothing happened. That used to make her feel great but this time, she was disappointed.

The skiff was lashed to the platform cleats temporarily allowing the Skipper and Peder to exit the skiff. Spica remained bobbing along side the Balaena.

No sooner did a soggy Hare step on board, the Skipper leaned down and whispered something in his ear.... Hare's expression and drooping ears told everyone that the Skipper's message was not pleasant.

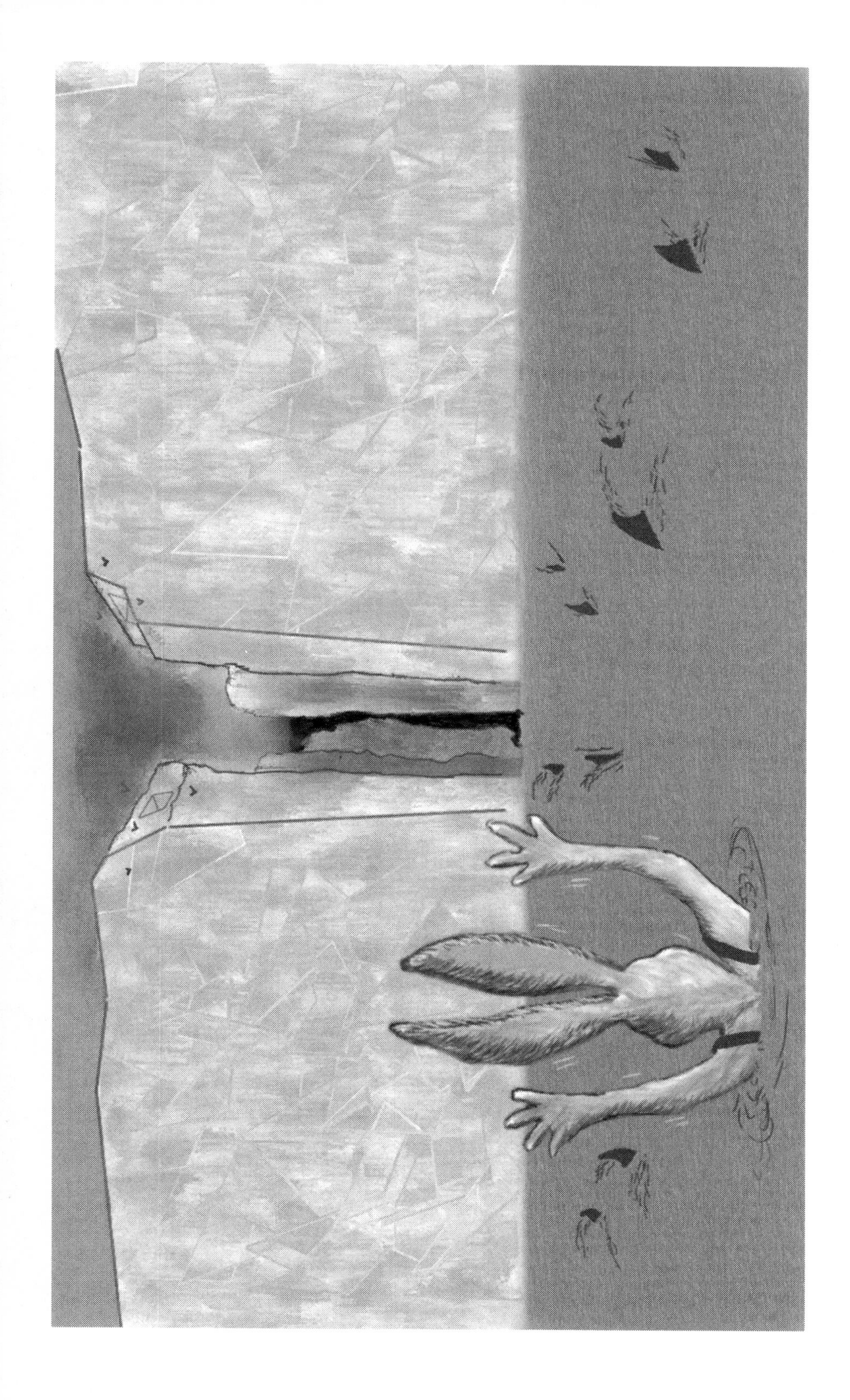

Chapter Twelve

Hare looked over at Hazel who was scowling at him. If he thought she was going to side with him or be sympathetic he was mistaken. He messed up big time and she wanted him to know it. She turned and walked away without words to once again join the Skipper on the bridge.

"Mr. Llars, Mr. Peder," ordered the Skipper, "please go below and break out another set of push-poles and the mizzen sail. We'll need about four folds of samson braid rope too. Take Mr. Hare with you and make sure he stays there. Seaman Hare, go with them please."

Hare looked at Hazel silently pleading for help but she nodded and said, "Harry, please do as instructed."

Hare didn't say anything but slowly followed Llars and Peder down below with his ears drooped more than ever.

Without much delay, Llars and Peder appeared back on deck and knew what the Skipper was planning.

As Hazel watched Llars and Peder wrap the heavy canvas sail tightly around the long push poles to make the bit, she asked the Skipper what he whispered to Hare.

"I told him the next time he pulls a stunt like that I'll feed him to the sharks m'self. Llars placed him in our brig way down below where it's cold and damp. I'll leave him there for a while to think about things."

"I'm sorry Skipper, I'll have a talk with him. He's just excited and perhaps too eager to-"

"....both of my son's were too eager as well."

Hazel had no rebuttal. She stood next to the Skipper in silence.

Meanwhile Hare was now in the brig, which on land would be called jail for lack of a more pleasant term. Normally he would have started crying like he did almost a week ago but he wasn't sobbing this time.

Hare was audibly swearing and under his breath cursing himself. He knew better but allowed himself to do it anyway. He naturally started pacing but couldn't pace far because his dank, moss lined, insect ridden, dungeon like cell was too small even for him.

Hazel-Mae was standing on the bridge watching Llars and Peder preparing the final step to making the bit. Skipper Eyvinn turned to her and said, "please take the conn my dear. I have to go help."

"Can I help instead?" asked Hazel, being uncomfortable about Hare's behavior.

"Thank you, no, "replied the Skipper, "I'll not have you turn your delicate hands into the lobster claws I have!"

The Skipper walked his way down to the bow to assist his crew. Hazel felt a very strong compulsion to go and talk to Hare but, 'taking the conn' meant that she was now the acting Skipper and in control of the ship. She stood as requested knowing the longer Hare was incarcerated the better. She was really mad at him anyway so this would allow her to let it simmer down a bit.

Hazel enjoyed the wonderful ocean breeze brushing her hair as she remained vigilant. She wasn't looking at what the crew was doing but was using the glass to survey their surroundings which was called, 'standing watch'. The last time she stood watch for Captain Eyvinn Hansen was many years ago; it felt good to be back at the Balaena's helm!

"That should do it Skip. What do you think Spica?" asked Peder.

Spica was more indestructible than shredder sharks so he didn't care, "looks good to me. It will fit nicely."

Hazel now looked down and saw a long cushioned bridle that had strong ropes tied to the port and starboard turnbuckles that would allow control over stress upon Spica.

Hazel continued to stand watch until the Skipper returned to the bridge. She smiled and said, "the adventure continues!"

"Yes it does but this will be a first for me," said the Skipper.

"Me too," replied Hazel.

The Skipper and Hazel watched Llars and Peder toss the improvised 'horse' bridle into the water. Taking into account Spica's total length plus another ten feet, allowed the colossal fish to swim into position and take the bit into it's mouth. Spica wiggled and flopped around to get the bit set in place comfortably.

Everyone felt the Balaena jolt forward as Spica tested the makeshift device and to the Skipper's elation, it would function as intended. Spica then backed out of his position and swam next to the Balaena.

“Good to go Skipper. Just remove your keel and we can proceed,” instructed Spica.

Llars and Peder were ready with goggles and the special tools they would need to detach the keel and hook it up to the winch. The process was easy since keel removal was a common task aboard this particular ship in these particular waters.

After the keel was secured, Llars gave the Skipper thumbs up who gave Spica the all clear to proceed.

The giant fish re-positioned himself with bit-in-mouth. Now the Balaena was under fish propulsion for the first time ever. As soon as they were moving, Llars returned to his station to man the stern rudder which would keep the rear of the ship somewhat stable. Peder would have to pull double-duty with the push-poles to keep the ship from scraping up against the narrow walls of the channel.

Everyone was at their station ready to slowly navigate their way through the erratically twisted corridor. The Balaena moved swiftly toward the channel opening when the Skipper held out a rusty key for Hazel.

“Please go below and free Seaman Hare as we will need all hands for this one!”

Hazel smiled broadly as she took the old key but as soon as she turned away her smile morphed into a frown.

Hare was going crazy feeling the ship move but he was behind bars. He was still cursing himself while wrapping his arms around himself to keep warm when he heard footsteps.

He expected the Skipper but saw Hazel instead. He could take the Captain's scorn but when he saw Hazel's expression, that was a different matter...

Hazel approached his cell and dangled the old rusty key in front of him. She didn't say anything until he tried to apologize.

Hare: “I am so sorry that...”

Hazel: “NO!”

Hare didn't turn away but stood still and looked directly at Hazel. This would be the first time he ever saw Hazel-Mae mad at him.

It was a classic stare-down that nobody won because there wasn't time as Hazel inserted the old key that took a while to work but finally allowed the rusted, neglected door to creak open.

Hare and Hazel stood facing each other when Hazel said in a very serious monotone, “Follow me.”

They walked up on deck when the bright sunlight blinded Hare. When he could see, he walked straight toward the Skipper.

“I have no excuse for my actions Skipper. It will not happen again,” said Hare looking directly at him.

“Yes, I know it won't.” The Skipper just glared at him then calmly replied, “please resume starboard push-pole duty Seaman.”

Hare didn't smile or show any emotion but simply answered orders, “aye-aye Skipper.”

Now all was ready to attempt the channel. Peder stood at the port side push pole, Hare stood ready at starboard, and Llars on the stern rudder. With the Skipper at the helm and Hazel at lookout with the glass, the Skipper was about to turn control of his ship over to a fish.

Skipper Eyvinn's big worry with this idea, which seemed to be their only option, was that without a keel, his ship would be like a loose cannon dangerously out of control. His ship was old and one good collision with a sharp, jagged channel wall could result in catastrophic disaster.

This is where he had to rely on the push-pole team to keep that from happening. Luckily, and oddly enough his greatest trust was with Spica; if anyone or anything knew these waters it would be a fish. Most importantly though was that he instinctively knew to pull the ship slowly.

Finally the opening to the channel was upon them as the Skipper issued a reminder, "STAND ALERT ALL HANDS, THIS IS GOING TO BE...."

Just then, a small school of dolphins shot past the ship and settled into an escort formation just ahead of Spica.

Hare wanted to break into his bunny dance seeing the dolphins but decided to use restraint. He stood firmly at his station concentrating on the task at hand. The Skipper and everyone else were very relieved because with the dolphins escorting the escort, the level of danger was now diminished and the Skipper's level of anxiety was cut by half.

Another problem still worried the Skipper though; Sheercliff Channel was not straight. It wound around creating blind spots which were even more difficult to see because now there was hardly any sunlight. On top of that, the Skipper couldn't speak to Spica to slow down or stop; he had no choice but to rely on a fishes judgment.

"You know how long I've been doing this," said the Skipper to Hazel, "I gotta say that I've never been more nervous."

"It's indeed a scenario I never could have imagined. Now I will tell you how disappointed I am in Harry. I apologize," said Hazel sincerely.

"My dear, please never apologize for the behavior of others. In many cases it's even beyond their control. I will say that crazy rabbit has some interesting friends. And, I must admit I like him; there's something special about him but any disregard for orders aboard this vessel or any other is unacceptable as it places everyone at risk. We are students of the sea and follow orders for a reason."

"You know I'm with you Skipper," said Hazel as she raised her spyglass.

The ship was being pulled slowly to the point where Hare could almost reach out and actually touch the wall to fend off the ship. He would watch Peder and emulate what he was doing to get proficient at it.

There was a point where the Balaena was actually moving around the twisting corridor smoothly which made the Skipper happy because although the channel was not that long, navigating in such a narrow passage was a very delicate operation especially without a keel.

Just around the time the Skipper was feeling confident this crazy maneuver might actually work, there were splashes from large rocks that hit the water and ricocheted off the corridor walls.

Hare nearly dropped his push pole being startled, “what was that?”

“WE HAVE THROWERS CAPTAIN,” alerted Peder!!!

“BLAST IT ALL,” yelled the Skipper waving his fist in the air, “I declare WAR on all of them; they killed my boy and I've had it, this must and WILL STOP.”

Hazel-Mae knew Eyvinn's two sons, Rolph and Karl. Rolph died due to drowning but Captain Eyvinn's first born, Karl, died as a result of injuries from being hit in the head with a large, jagged rock tossed over by a thrower. Many don't see Hazel-Mae really angry but she knew the Skipper was right, something had to be done.

No one could ever get a look at who or what was responsible for tossing boulders over the high cliffs but Hazel knew of many deaths and injuries caused by it. The time had come to finally eliminate this terrible threat.

“I have this Skipper, better cover your ears.” Hazel cupped her hands over her mouth and let out a shrill cry that seemed to echo across the flat water and into the surrounding forests. Suddenly the boulders stopped raining down on them. Hazel knew it wouldn't be that easy.

“What did you do?” asked the Skipper.

“..... called in the air force.”

Just then another larger boulder hit the channel wall literally breaking in half sending a sharp shard of shrapnel slicing Peder's arm. Hare wanted to help but had to stay at his post to protect the ship.

Skipper Eyvinn turned the conn over to Hazel again as he rushed off the bridge to assist Peder who was bleeding badly.

She watched Skipper Eyvinn help Peder down below for medical treatment. Hare instantly picked up both push-poles doing double duty which pleased Hazel but now Hare was in danger.

She looked behind her and saw Llars working the rudder obviously concerned about his ship mate. Spica and the dolphin escort could feel and sense each boulder hitting the water but couldn't do anything about it.

Hazel had never been Captain of a ship in such a dire situation. The boulders kept raining down upon them and if that weren't enough, they had to keep moving otherwise they'd not only be a sitting duck but also dead in the water.

Hazel remained on the bridge doing her best to keep it all together when another boulder not only hit the ship but took out a large chunk of the port bow which was just enough for the Balaena to begin taking on water.

Hare was almost hit by the splintering wood and stone shards but stood his post not about to give up. Skipper Eyvinn and a wounded Peder suddenly appeared on deck. Peder ran to his station to check on Hare while the Captain relieved Hazel on the bridge.

Peder was badly injured, holding his right forearm and bleeding through his bandages, but tried to take his post when Hare yelled out to him over the chaos for all to hear...

“No Peder, you have one good arm, go relieve Llars on the rudder so he can go below and check for damage. I have this. Go!”

The Skipper slowly looked over at Hazel with his mouth dropped open....”that was going to be my exact order...”

Just then Hare yelled even louder, “please check on our ponies too.”

Hazel chuckled despite their current situation, “I did say he'd surprise you! Go check down below with Llars Captain, I have the conn.”

“...right, yes indeed. Watch yourself.” Skipper Eyvinn was temporarily stunned by the sudden change in decisions coming from everyone but him though suddenly felt as if they would get through this.

The Skipper hurried down below to the forecastle where there were living quarters and dry storage holds. Llars was the first to arrive at the damaged area.

“Skip, it's not too bad but we'll have to alter ballast otherwise we will eventually sink but-”

Just then there were several large splashes enough to move the ship but it wasn't caused by boulders. Hazel-Mae was yelling as the Skipper and Llars both rushed top-side.

They arrived on deck to see a massive curtain of Bousterama's quarter flock filling the high, narrow slice of air between both sides of the channel. Rama's air force had picked up the throwers and tossed them over the cliff. There seemed to be dead, floating throwers everywhere and the Balaena was still moving.

“ALL STOP...”, ordered the Skipper but he forgot it was not up to him.

Hare was happy to see his feathered friends again but had to stop the ship. He thought for a second and took charge... again.

“Llars,” yelled Hare, “help me here!”

Llars was wondering what to do as he looked over at Skipper Eyvinn. The Skipper simply said, “Go!”

Llars got to Hare who instructed him to take one rope while he would take the other then pull gently telling Spica to stop. Hare figured that these guys knew the sea but he knew the land. Riding Belle gave him the idea that Spica could be a water-pony so he just improvised - like any good musician!

“Ready?” asked Hare looking seriously at Llars.

“Ready...”

Hare said intently, “pull slowly but at the same time, okay? One, two, and...”

They both yanked back the rope at the same time which proved what a beast-fish Spica truly was but it worked. Spica, slowed to a stop. He detached himself from the bridle and swam carefully toward the Balaena as did the dolphins.

Spica could now see what happened. The dolphins surrounded the area as lookouts for sharks as the Skipper noticed Spica's expression.

“You've had issues with the throwers too I see.”

“Yes Skipper, I have. Look right at the base of my dorsal. See that indentation? I wondered if I'd ever be able to swim efficiently again.”

“It's my ship but your ocean,” said the Skipper, “what do you want to do with this mess of evil nasties?”

“Let them feed the ocean,” answered Spica, “they have terrorized this channel for far too long. I say let them float until the shredders arrive. I want to get out of this area right away; I feel movement and it's not throwers.”

“The channel is moving closer as we sit here,” said Hazel, “we should make haste.”

“Yes,” said the Skipper, “immediately because we are likely to see retribution from the throwers that remain.”

Hazel reminded the Skipper, “Captain Eyvinn, if Rama's flock is here there won't be any.”

Chapter Thirteen

Hare didn't have a problem convincing Skipper Eyvinn he could pull double duty fending off the ship despite having been thrown in the brig. Skipper Eyvinn watched him take charge and perhaps not only saved the ship but Peder as well.

The Skipper relieved Hazel from the bridge which allowed her to go below to work her magic treating Peder properly. From the Skipper's fly-bridge vantage point he saw Hare ready with double push poles amidships, Llars was manning the stern rudder, Spica was pulling the Balaena slowly but effortlessly thanks to the five dolphin escort, while he was at the helm. The Skipper smiled knowing all was well.

Without further threats from throwers, the Balaena moved slowly along as all hands worked efficiently to finally guide the ship to where the channel opened up. Hare could see the open bay ahead and silently released a deep sigh. This would allow them to come to a complete stop which was necessary to get the Balaena back to normal operation. Just then, Hazel and Peder appeared topside with Peder out of his sling and ready to resume his duties.

Spica was finally released from his task as the Balaena was refitted with her keel and the steam engine lit. The dolphins continued to swim around as guards while Skipper Eyvinn called a meeting with the crew.

“First of all,” said the Skipper smiling,”thank you all for your courage and outstanding resilience under extreme, shall we say, duress.” The Skipper then altered his expression to a scowl, “secondly, Seaman Harry front and center immediately.”

Hare was still holding both push-poles which he carefully placed on the deck and approached the Skipper ready to accept a well deserved tongue-lashing.

“Seaman Harrison Hare, you are in violation of title 10, section 892, article 92 of the Sailor's Code specifically citing you with, 'dereliction of duty', or willfully refusing to follow orders. How do you plead sir?”

“Guilty as charged Skipper. I have no excuse.” said Hare owning what he did.

“Very well. I have no choice then but,” the Skipper pulled out a medal from his back pocket placing it over Hare's long ears and around his neck, “to promote you to honorary Lieutenant Commander of the Balaena for taking charge under fire which, in my view, not only resulted in a successful mission but you put the safety of your shipmate before yourself. Congratulations Lt. Commander Harrison Hare! You can sail with us anytime!”

The Skipper then stood before Lt. Cmdr. Hare and actually saluted him as did Llars, and Hazel, Peder just nodded.

Everyone then applauded Hare who was stunned to say the least. Hazel was nearly in tears but was surprised he didn't initiate a serious bunny-dance. He stood there looking down at the gleaming award then freaked out yanking it from around his neck throwing it to the deck!

Everyone but Hazel-Mae gasped, especially the Skipper. Hare backed off with a terrified expression on his face. Hazel intervened-

“Its okay Harry, its -”. She looked over at the even more wide-eyed Lemuriped crew and explained. “The last time he had something hanging around his neck, he -”

Hazel stopped short looking over at Hare raising her eyebrows. Hare slowly nodded, 'yes', giving her permission to briefly tell the story.

“- he had his trumpet hanging around his neck when we crossed Snake Gorge. He was waving his arms around to find his balance and his arm got caught in the strap and, well... over he went.”

Hare had to say something. “I.... I am so sorry,” stammered Hare who walked over to the medal picking it up. He gently blew the dust off of it then held it to his heart, “I meant no disrespect. I now have a second prized possession...” Hare now attempted to talk through welling tears, “my father's prized trumpet is my first, this is my second. Thank you. Thank you from the bottom of my heart.”

The Balaena crew stood motionless upon hearing that he actually fell into the gorge yet lived to tell about it. Hare then snapped out it and decided to add some levity to the drama...

“Okay, enough of that. So,” asked Hare with a sly grin, holding up his shining medal, “as an *honorary* lieutenant commander, may I issue an order?”

The Skipper laughed and walked over to his new officer placing his large hand on Hare's shoulder, “yes sir Commander Harry, you may.”

“Okay,” said Hare trying to imitate the Skipper which even made him laugh, “my order is to drop anchor and everybody have some fun! Let's get some seafood, some music and some singing going on! We have all earned a good time!”

The Skipper and especially Peder who was still sore but could clap began applauding! The Skipper then boomed out *his* order, “plot a course to Reef Cove. Stations please!”

The keel had been replaced, tightened and re-aligned and the steam engine was ready to fire-up. Three bells were heard as Llars began to shovel the purple coal into the chute. Before long, the Balaena easily followed Spica and the ever present dolphin escort led the way around the maze of coral reefs.

It was now mid afternoon when the Balaena finally approached the end of the channel. This would open up an amazing panorama of the incredibly beautiful Low Valley Timbers Bay, called Timber Bay for short.

Peder now joined Hare on deck for push-pole duty. Although it wasn't needed now, it would be shortly since they were approaching what was known as Twin Horn.

Twin Horn was important because it not only marked the end of the dangerous channel but also meant Reef Cove was literally right around the corner.

There could still be sneaky throwers that remained undetected by Rama's scout birds but that was a long shot. Soon the channel land mass would drift tightly closed forever forcing the brutal and remorseless thrower gang to seek new ground elsewhere.

The best thing about Reef Cove was that unlike normal coves, this one was covered, like a half cave. The Balaena's mast height fit perfectly under the natural canopy and was one of the Skipper's regular retreats.

Skipper Eyvinn was pleased, and relieved to shout out his order, "TWIN HORN APPROACHING. STAND ALERT ALL HANDS!"

Peder and Hare were ready with their push-poles because the distance between twin horn was so narrow they once again had to extinguish the engine and coast with oars at the ready.

The momentum they produced allowed the Balaena to smoothly pass through the narrow twin horn passage with ease which also allowed the Skipper to enjoy a significant sigh of relief!

Without being told, Peder and Hare went below to release the port and starboard oars which would be their only propulsion. From down below where the oar station was, you couldn't see where you were going. Peder was comfortable with this but Hare was nervous. Peder made it simple...

"We just make the ship go. The Skipper and Llars steer it and with your huge fish friend and the dolphins, there's nothing to worry about. Just remember when we're set for mooring, drop the anchor."

"Got it!" said Hare excited.

It didn't take long before the Balaena was carefully guided around the first coral reef. They finally drifted effortlessly into Reef Cove as Skipper Eyvinn ordered "all stop."

Peder and Hare stowed the oars and high-fived each other as they appeared top-side. Hare gasped at the sight he was now looking at! Peder was watching him because he had been here many times but for Hare, to see this particular sight from within Reef Cove was a living picture right out of a dream!

Hare stood there dumbfounded, just staring out at the breathtaking beauty.

He looked up at the bridge and shouted, "it's amazing! I could live here!"

Hazel laughed and turned to the Skipper, "he's been saying that about every place he's seen!"

“Can't blame him,” said the Skipper, “there are many beautiful areas in your territory my dear, on land and off, and this is just one! Please excuse me, time for a walk-around.”

“Aye, aye, Skip,” answered Hazel, “I have the conn.”

As the Skipper made his way below, he turned and said, “there is no conn to have my dear! Relax, it's time to enjoy the peace and quiet of this beautiful cove!”

The Skipper made his rounds inspecting their position and especially the damage caused by the throwers. Meanwhile Hazel was returning the fly-bridge to ship-shape condition as Peder and Hare straightened up the deck where thrower debris remained. Hare noticed Peder's arm was okay but still bled slightly through the bandage.

“We should change that bandage,” said Hare.

“No need. Us Lemur-types are pretty tough critters. It'll be okay. Thanks for your concern!”

Hare heard a loud metallic sound and turned just in time to see the entire engine platform lower slowly down into the stern hold. The large deck doors were secured leaving a huge open deck now available for their celebration!

Soon the Skipper and Llars appeared back on deck...

“Everything ship shape Mr. Peder?”

Peder and Hare looked at each other when Peder said, “you say it!”

“Aye-aye Skipper, anchor is away,” shouted Lt. Cmdr. Hare.

“Thank you Commander Harry. But it's pronounced 'aweigh', not away!”

“Thank you Captain, however - “...

Hare decided it was time to start the show! He thought up a quick rap to begin:

Aweigh and away both sound the same,

I didn't know that but I'm not to blame,

Never been on a ship but you gave me a chance,

So now it's time for your first bunny-dance!"

Hare's ears were flapping and each one doing it's own thing while his big, huge feet were slapping the deck to his own silent rhythm. His expressions were just silly as he'd do his wiggling-rabbit-nose-thing and crossing his eyes!

Both Peder and Llars began cracking up because that was not proper answering to a Captain. Of course, seeing Skipper Eyvinn almost fall overboard laughing, was the signal for their party to begin!

...and once again, Hare took charge! "Do you guys have any musical instruments laying around?"

The Skipper instantly got up and disappeared below, as did Peder. Llars started to clap knowing what was about to occur. Hazel then got up and smiled at Hare asking him-

"Brand new or kick around?"

Hare was still tapping his long foot rubbing his chin thinking, "lets go with both!"

"Aye, aye Commander," said Hazel as she turned to join the Skipper and Peder down in the hold.

Hare was excited to finally have a chance to play. Just as he was wondering what instruments the Skipper and Peder would bring, they appeared on deck as Hare started to jump up and down!

"Wow! A violin! And a guitar? This is going to be great," exclaimed Hare as he scampered over to where Hazel placed both of his trumpets.

Meanwhile, as Hare was in serious deliberation now about which bell he wanted to start with, the Skipper was the first to rosin up his bow

and begin playing. Hare abruptly stopped and listened to the Skipper. He slowly looked over at Hazel who was smiling, knowing the Skipper was classically trained. Just then, Peder joined him with a guitar backup that sent chills up Hare's spine!

The one thing that made it sound so good were the acoustics in the cove, but it was pleasantly obvious that the Skipper and Peder had played many times before.

They continued to get 'loosened up' since it had been a while since the two jammed but Hare picked out his kick-around bell and just listened to get a feel for where the tune was going.

Just then Hare looked over at Llars, “aren't you going to join in?”

Llars laughed, “sorry, these guys have the talent, not me.”

“Well you can hum along can't you?”

“I think I'll just sit back and enjoy the jam,” said Llars. “Thanks anyway.”

“Okay, “said Hare, “wish me luck pal, I'm just a beginner!”

“I'm sure you'll do fine Commander!”

Hare laughed and went over to where the Skipper was standing.

The Skipper and Peder continued to warm up as Hazel knew the melody and sang a beautiful harmony. This got Hare serious as he intently listened to the trio building in tempo and proficiency. Hare raised his trumpet and joined in with long, steady notes that seemed to bind the entire sound together. Hare still hit some sour notes but for a beginner, his particular style made even the mistakes sound acceptable!

Right when they began sounding as if they've been rehearsing for weeks, the Skipper stood up and started to solo, showing off just how good his violin skills were! Hare stopped playing, as did Peder allowing the Skipper to shred, and shred he did!

The Skipper finished his improv-solo which deserved a standing ovation by everyone. This is also when Hare saw a very different side to the always-serious Captain Eyvinn Hansen!

"Thank you, thank you all! Astounding! I can't believe these old strings are actually still in tune! That was fun. Nice trumpet work Commander," complimented the Skipper.

Hare chuckled, "thank you Skipper but let's just go with Harry from now on if that's okay!"

"That be fine with me Harry," chuckled the Skipper.

Hare interjected, "hey Skip, what was that song you were singing early this morning before it got light?"

The Skipper laughed but Peder answered, "that would be 'the endless journey", one of my favorites to hear and to play!"

"Thank you for that Mr. Peder," the Skipper looked over at Hare, "wanna work on that one?"

"Sure," answered Hare, "but you guys go ahead and play it through so I can get a better feel for it.

The Skipper nodded at Peder, "Peder starts this one off since it's not easy to sing with a violin beneath the chin! Ready Peder?"

Peder started the guitar progression while turning to Hare, "I'm in the open key of G major at three/four time."

"Aye-aye dude," said Hare already tapping his foot!

The Skipper cleared his already raspy throat then gave Peder a nod...

I come from a long-long line o' smelly skippers,

From sloops, ketches, and rotted clippers,

I've 'et barnacle stew and drank shark-blood tea,

That's why this is the only life for me,

I want salt in my face and the wind at my back,

To hear the brass bell toll and the canvas crack,

Taking me to another distant shore,

Where I can sail on and find a thousand more....

The Skipper stopped singing to instruct his audience, “this is the chorus so everybody sing along!”

So its Aye-Aye mates, keep the horizon in sight,

Then read the stars until mornings light,

Onward we sail, to meet new friends,

Aye-Aye mates, our journey never ends,

Bring me the typhoon's rain, that I know will fall,

The giant squids, lighting strikes, I'll take it all,

I'll brave hurricanes, hail, and other nasties from the deep,

Because thar be more ports o' call b'fore I sleep,

I've had many loves lost to the merciless sea,

My wife, my boy's, and my serenity,

But this life chose me, its my fate to roam,

To every shore till the sea takes my bones,

The Skipper reminded everyone, “sing along time now kiddies...”

So its Aye-Aye mates, keep the horizon in sight,

Then read the stars until mornings light,

Onward we sail, to meet new friends,

Aye-Aye mates, our journey never ends.

Peder finished the last strum as the Skipper took a drink of water. Hare stood motionless! He was amazed how the Skipper's gruff sounding speaking voice was the exact opposite of his smooth, unwavering singing voice.

“That was great!” exclaimed Hare applauding. “I love that tune! Let's do it again!”

The Skipper smiled while unconsciously sawing out a quick riff , “you really like that tune?”

“Well duh Skip! Yeah, love the lyrics and cool chord progression too...”

Peder started laughing listening to the way Hare spoke to the Skipper. He had never heard such 'loose' language spoken to his Captain – ever! But Skipper Eyvinn loved it! Even Spica and the dolphins were listening to the song and swam around playing!

“Okay,” said Hare suddenly becoming the musical director,” you guys just do the same thing, don't change a note! I'd like to try something. Just play and I'll come in whenever. Cool? Alright man here we go, from the top please!”

Peder began the guitar intro but Skipper Eyvinn waited for Hare to add to it. Peder's consistent rhythm guitar set the stage for Hare to fill in with a low register as they both were watching Eyvinn. He finally nodded then abruptly stopped.

“No, no,” said Eyvinn, “let's just play. I'll sing next time maybe. I want to play and your trumpet sounds great with us. So, let's jam a bit!"

Hare smiled as did Peder since Skipper Eyvinn's prowess on the violin was always a joy to play with. Peder's guitar was slightly out of tune due to it's bowed neck but good enough to set a rhythm everyone could follow. Between the guitar, trumpet, and Cappy's violin, the boys played whatever they felt like up until dusk when they finally stopped.

As night fell over the calm serenity of Reef Cove, the current crew of the Balaena sat and ate, laughed, and traded stories until everyone fell asleep... everyone but Hare.

Chapter Fourteen

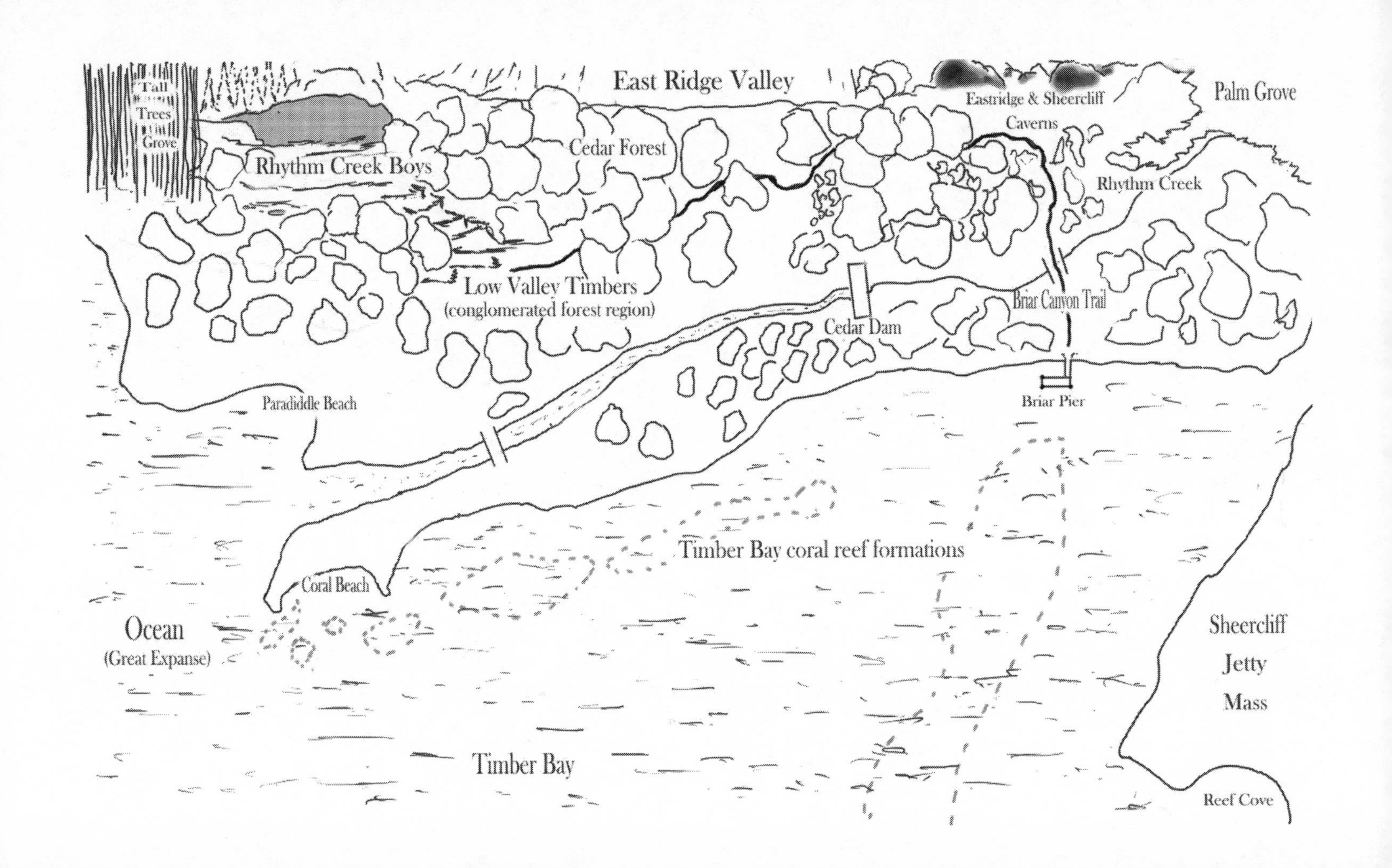
Tall
Trees
Grove
East Ridge Valley
Eastridge & Sheercliff
Caverns
Palm Grove
Cedar Forest
Rhythm Creek Boys
Rhythm Creek
Low Valley Timbers
(conglomerated forest region)
Briar Canyon Trail
Cedar Dam
Paradiddle Beach
Briar Pier
Timber Bay coral reef formations
Coral Beach
Ocean
(Great Expanse)
Sheercliff
Jetty
Mass
Timber Bay
Reef Cove

Knowing how close to Rhythm Creek they were, Hare had a hard time trying to sleep but he eventually drifted off. He was awakened by the ship bumping up against the dock but quickly faded back to sleep. Half an hour went by when Hare flew out of his bedroll now thinking it wasn't a dream and what he felt were throwers. He hurried topside ready for anything.

No sooner did he appear on deck, Hare was surprised by an amazing breakfast spread out on a table standing where the steam engine used to be. Llars was the first to see him.

“There he is! Come join us Harry! The Skipper was about to go wake you up with a cup of cold water in the face! He likes doing that if you sleep in!”

“Well,” said Hare smiling, “I would have deserved it! What did I miss? Oh wow, look at this,” exclaimed Hare as he gazed down at the delectable feast! He began jumping up and down... “you have eggs!!! I haven't had an egg for.... wow, and bacon, and...pastries, and.... carrot-potato pie??? Oh man, why did you let me sleep in? This is amazing! Who prepared all of this?”

Hazel-Mae pointed at Llars, “the guy with the apron! The Balaena's very own Master Chef!”

Hare looked over at Llars, “what's all this stuff about having no talent?”

“I may be tone deaf but if you like to eat, I'm the guy to see! Do you want to eat?” asked Llars.

Hare immediately answered, “Of course!”

“One question first, “asked Llars...

“... okay,” said Hare.

“What-cha-waitin' for?!!?”

Hare rubbed his hands together and was about to sit down when he stopped abruptly.

“Wait a second. I forgot something.” Hare rushed down below and seconds later returned with his medal hanging around his neck.

“There, now I can officially enjoy breakfast,” announced Hare standing at his seat doing a quick bunny dance! This had become a favorite with the Skipper and never ceased to make him laugh. Finally, all antics aside, Hare sat down and dove into this wonderful meal.

Hare never felt better! Deep inside though, he knew the empty feeling of saying goodbye to new friends was not only inevitable but drawing closer. He'd fret over that later. Right now, he was going to enjoy the savory feast while relishing the breath-taking view of their surroundings.

Like the night before, they all sat on the wide open deck eating, telling stories, and laughing! Every now and then the Skipper would stand up and break into song. Like us all, he also had a silly side to him and made Hare laugh so hard he nearly fell off the barrel he was sitting on!

Hare was still laughing when he noticed Spica and the dolphins were gone. He began to lower his ears, disappointed, but then perked up as he realized that they had their own lives and simply had to move on. Hazel-Mae noticed his change of expression.

“Spica asked me to tell you what an adventure it was and he hopes to see you again sometime... and thanks for saving his life.”

“I wish I could have said goodbye. But, that's okay. One day I'll return here and hopefully I can find him. I just wonder how long that will be.”

Meanwhile, Peder and Hazel were helping Llars clean up as Llars kept an immaculate galley. The Skipper was down below double checking on the damage to the forecastle as Hare appeared.

“Hello Harry! Llars cooks up some mean chow does he not?”

“The best! That was a delicious surprise.”

“What's on your mind Harry?” asked the Skipper.

“How long are you going to be docked here?”

"We're planning to shove off in roughly an hour. Llars and Peder are making the galley ship-shape and I'm checking our rough patch here for leakage. Why?"

"Remember when I told you about the big jam event at my place in the Glade? I'd like to remind you of the invitation."

The Skipper stopped working and said while wiping his hands, "that will do it. Now we won't sink. Okay, what? Oh, yes-" He looked at Hare smiling.

"I hate to be blunt Harry, but that won't happen. I'm truly sorry, but it's too far inland and we have many important appointments. But, I will repeat my promise to you that you can sail with us anytime you're back in this area again. But, before we shove off, wanna jam one more song? I really like your fills!"

Hare jumped up and down! "Really? Thank you Skip. Did you write the song?"

"Yes I did, many years ago."

"Cool! If this will be our last jam, let's get to it!"

"Well my friend, hopefully this won't be our last jam. C'mon, lets go up top and get busy!"

After the Skipper knew the Balaena was seaworthy and was ready for their next voyage, he gathered everyone for one last song before they disembarked.

The Skipper cleared his throat..." This song is called 'Life's irony'. The tune is in common time in the key of D."

Hare stood ready, as before, to find where he had to be and to get a feeling for the tune. Peder began and their wonderful sound floated across the calm bay for all to hear.

Oh how I long for the days of old,

That restless youth with a pinch of gold,

Life was so simple, so carefree and wild,

The air was sweet, and the ocean mild,

Our paths were always open and free,

Thar be no barriers upon the open sea,

To many foreign lands I did roam,

And many of them I did call home,

But nothing moves faster than the slow hands of time,

Your minds works slowly and simple words won't rhyme,

Years pass like minutes, and days speed by,

Before you're aware, it's time to say goodbye,

Oh how I long for the days of old,

The friends I met and the hearts I stole,

One of those hearts was my dear wife,

Who gave me two sons that lost their lives,

So maybe that's the lesson I now give,

Take the good with the bad and learn how to live,

Live helping others with kindness and truth,

And don't ever worry about losing your youth,

Nothing moves faster than the slow hands of time,

Today life's a mess, tomorrow it's sublime,

Wisdom will be yours, but only time will tell,

If you have learned all your life lessons well.

The song was played several times in different ways, but everyone knew it would be a fleeting moment. Finally, all instruments were put away, and emotional goodbyes were said through hugs, tears, and handshakes. Blaze and Belle were gently unloaded from the hold then placed on land. Everyone was re-supplied with provisions and fresh water when the Balaena finally did shove off.

Hazel and Hare stood on Briar Pier listening to the Skipper sing his, "Endless Journey" song while Hare played along with it as loud as he could. He eventually stopped playing as they watched the Balaena slowly disappear into the foggy haze heading across the bay toward the endless freedom of the great expanse.

Suddenly way off in the distance, Hare heard the report of the signal cannon! He jumped up in his saddle laughing! "Ha! I completely forgot about wanting to fire that thing off. Farewell my friends," said Hare saluting," many, many thanks."

Hazel smiled then asked him, "why do you think you forgot about firing the cannon? I know you really wanted to."

"I don't know.... it just wasn't important anymore I guess," Hare started humming one of the Skipper's songs as Hazel also joined in.

Before too long they stopped humming when Hare asked, "So, we're almost there; think I'm good enough to jam with these guys?"

"Are you kidding? You'll do awesome Harry! I have seen you grow in so many ways and it's only been eight days! That's astonishing! And let us not forget that you cheated death not once but twice! Wait until I tell them, they won't believe it!"

“You know, please promise not to say anything about Snake gorge or the sharks,” said Hare.

“Okay, I promise, but why? Its amazing enough to happen once but twice to the same guy within days of each other? No one else out there could claim that.”

“Yes, and that's my point. No one out there would claim to be *that* accident prone. Really though, this whole incredible journey we have been on was always about the music, so that's all I want to concentrate on. Nothing else matters. Soon we'll be there and that will be the end of the musical quest of Harrison Hare!”

Hazel laughed. “Aren't you forgetting something?”

Hare thought and scrunched up his face in bewilderment, “I don't think so. What could I be forgetting?”

“You still have to get home.”

Chapter Fifteen

Hare didn't say anything but looked puzzled as they rode through the lush timbers that split the Briar Canyon trail. He realized that Hazel was right, he did forget about getting home. He then further realized he wasn't sure when he would see his home again since he didn't know how long he would be at Rhythm Creek. Suddenly many questions presented themselves which led to Hare's silence.

Hazel was silent also as she was immersed in her own thoughts. She knew Hare would do well. After everything he's already been through on their journey, the time had come for Hare to channel that knowledge and then concentrate on the many new lessons he would soon have to learn, digest, then practice.

Just then Hare started humming again, then sang quietly:

Hmmm, hmmm, hmm, hmm,

I come from a long line of smelly skippers, from sloops, ketches, and rotted clippers,

Hazel then joined in:

I've 'et barnacle stew and drank shark-blood tea, that's why this is the only life for me....

Hazel was going to keep singing but Hare decided to abruptly change the subject.

“How long will I be at Rhythm Creek do you think?”

“That, Harry, is up to you,” replied Hazel. “When you get to the point when you're satisfied with your progress, say the word and I'll be contacted. Then we'll plan your route home.”

“You'll be contacted? What does that mean? Are you going somewhere?”

“Yes of course. As soon as you're settled in with the band, I have business that has become long overdue.”

“I understand. I'm still overwhelmed at everything you've done for me. Why did you go through all that trouble by the way?”

“No trouble Harry, it's what I do. Much of my territory is untamed so it requires constant attention and communication with the clan leaders so I'm able to help where needed. When Yungbuck told Owl, who then told me what happened when you ran away, it was my responsibility to put this journey in motion... and I wanted to anyway! My big worry was wondering if you'd even want to go.”

“Well, your timing was perfect because I didn't feel wanted. I felt alone so I just ran away. Dumb thing to do but it did lead to right now! But we've said that everything happens for a reason, so maybe me running off like I did was a good thing. Maybe I was just bored. Or maybe I was-”.

Hazel interrupted, “yes Harry! You were bored because you were growing up! The things you used to love doing were boring to you because your mind was growing. You, were growing! You just needed direction which was my job!”

“And I can't thank you enough. So, you think I'm ready for this?”

“You better be, because we're here!”

They took the west route that ran parallel to Rhythm Creek that would take them right to the band's front door. But before they could get there, they had to be very careful to watch the road ahead of them. Most travelers here for the first time get into accidents because they're entranced by the beauty of Cedar Forest.

They rode along as Hare was practicing with Hazel humming along when suddenly Hare stopped and sat astonished in his saddle.

“Wow!!!”

“Told you,” said Hazel with a big smile! “Remember when I told you about all the many different varieties of trees growing in the same area? It all started here! It's as if someone deliberately planted every variety they could find right here and it spread.”

“The colors are amazing! I've never seen anything like it,” said Hare still wide-eyed! The forest jambalaya boasted a full spectrum of enchantment Hare couldn't have imagined.

They rode slowly as they passed the entrance of Cedar Forest as Hazel pointed around.

"Right there, you have the golden bronze color of the hickory. Behind that grove you can barely make out the red/browns of the oak. The purple and red you see are dogwood, and the bright yellows are the birch, rainbow maple, redwoods, pines, ferns, spruces off in the distance, but mostly cedars. Oh, and not to mention the palm grove over there where the trail ended. Yes Harry, you will love living here!"

"You bet I will! There must be every kind of tree in the world right here," said Hare, "well, every tree except bamboo."

"You like bamboo? Just wait! Our craftspeople built the drum set you will soon see. Just like the set Duggle plays but custom made since the Chimpanzees are much bigger than we are! They used the bamboo from the grove right here in their own backyard. It's a hike to get to but they'll show you one day."

"Blazin' bell, what kind of trees are those really tall ones?"

"Those are called Stick Willows. They are indigenous to this area as far as I know. I travel to all corners of this territory and I've never seen them anywhere else. They're average height is around 50 feet but can surpass that."

"How come they don't have leaves?"

"My, aren't you observant?"

"Being observant is easy when they're the only trees I can see with no leaves!"

"Well, they never have leaves, hence the name, *stick* willow. If you get close up, you'll see tiny hairs covering the trunk and branches, like a fuzzy sweater. That's how they breathe."

"Trees don't breathe, c'mon you're messin' with me again!"

"Well sure they do Harry! We breath in oxygen and exhale carbon dioxide. Trees breath in what we exhale and when they exhale they give off oxygen. Some call it the circle of life while scientists call it respiration. Just ask Oakmaster!"

"No, no, that won't be necessary, I believe you! We learn something new everyday don't we?"

"Yes, if we listen and pay attention. Want to know what the best thing about stick willows is?"

"I'm all ears!"

"The Tall Trees Grove marks the entrance to the band's cave! We will be there in moments!!!"

Hazel-Mae and Hare with horn in hand at long last reached the East Ridge which did appear to be a jungle instead of a forest. There was a huge cave opening at the mountain's base shrouded in lush growth surrounded by some of the tallest trees Hare had ever seen.

As they approached the large opening, Hare was so relieved to see the band's front door, he raised his trumpet to let them know they had arrived. Before he could get a note off, Hare heard rustling above them that could only mean one thing!

Instantly a large chimpanzee seemed to fall from the sky, "What's up friends?"

Hare and the ponies were startled as a large chimpanzee just fell from the sky and was suddenly standing in front of them. Hazel-Mae went up to the chimpanzee and hugged him.

"Mombo, it is awesome to see you! How are things? It's been a while," said Hazel-Mae.

"My Lady Hazel-Mae, it's been too long! Who do we have here? I see that you've brought us a horn player. How cool is that?" said Mombo.

"Mombo meet Harrison Hare. Harry meet Mombo... the coolest cat to ever beat them skins!" said Hazel.

"Hi Mombo," replied Hare.

“Greeting my long eared rabbit friend! Welcome to Rhythm Creek where the jams never stop! C'mon and meet the band,” said Mombo as he led them into the main gallery.

Hare and Hazel-Mae followed Mombo into the cave where after a short walk they arrived at a large, flat gallery where there were musical instruments everywhere. There were guitars of all different types, a set of drums, a piano, and other instruments. Hare could only stand there and look in amazement. Mombo held both arms out as a welcoming gesture as Hazel-Mae watched Hare's expression.

“This is incredible”, said Hare as he just stood and stared, “I’ve never seen anything like it.”

“Not a bad set up huh?”, replied Mombo. “Man, we got it goin’ on down here. Every night’s a jam and sometimes we'll play live events! Let me get the crew for ya.”

Mombo walked over and sat down at the drums and began a drum solo like Hare had never heard. This guy was really good! After a few minutes, four other chimpanzees entered the room from different hallways and they all greeted Hazel-Mae with hugs and laughter! It was like a reunion when Mombo stopped his drumming and walked over to introduce everyone to Hare.

“Guys, I want you to meet our new horn man, Harry. This here is Wombat, our intense bass-ape, over there is Bombo our main guitar chimp, next to him is Little Kong who plays a mean blues harp, and finally we have Chimpzilla who shreds on the keyboard.”

They all gathered around Hare an made him feel right at home.

“Hi fella's,” said Hare smiling. “nice to meet you! Be warned that I'm a beginner and just started to play so I'm not in your caliber. But, I am here to learn and appreciate your efforts on my behalf. I promise to do the best that I can.”

“Hey man,” said Chimpzilla, “we all have to start somewhere so grab that bell and let's get to jammin!”

Hare turned to ask Hazel-Mae something but she was gone. He

looked around and was about to go outside to look for her.

Mombo saw his confused expression. “Don't worry about Hazel, she does that pal. One second she's here then the next she's off doing her good work. You will see her again but she would agree that she can't teach you what we can.”

“Zilla had a great idea,” said Mombo, “pick up that bell and let's see where we stand!”

Hare wasted no time filling that request.

Hare lived with the chimpanzees for years, almost forgetting about his nice, warm, comfortable home in the glade. One day, right in the middle of their mid-day jam, he stopped abruptly and Chimpzilla noticed that he was fidgeting and not being himself.

“What’s up with your nervous self Harry?” said Chimpzilla.

“I was just thinking that I haven’t been home in years. I wonder if I still have a home. Owl said they would look after my place but it’s been so long. They might think I’m dead or something awful,” said Hare.

Mombo was sitting next to him and shook his head up and down expecting this. He noticed a change in Hare weeks ago but just didn't say anything. He put his sticks down and walked over to Hare placing his arm around his shoulders.

“My brother, you must do what’s in your heart man. Hazel-Mae taught you that. If it's time for you to return home, you must do it. But you will not be going alone, right Zilla?”

“Harry, we will always be brothers, you know, family,” said Chimpzilla. “And family doesn't just say, it's been fun, see ya. So we have this idea to play a concert in your home town and, you know, stir things up a little!”

“Really? You guys would go through all that trouble for me?”

“No trouble for family Harry,” reiterated Zilla. “We love ya buddy.”

Hare cried and laughed at the same time being overcome with emotion. He had come to love his chimpanzee brothers and threw his arms around Mombo. Wombat, Chimpzilla, Bombo, and Little Kong, all gathered around him. They all knew it was time for Hare to return home.

After Hare's emotional outburst, he rallied the band together feeling better to resume their usual after-breakfast jam but their groove just wasn't there. They all felt it and as the last note was played, Hare lowered the horn and sat down. He was exhausted, but not from playing.

Mombo put down his sticks, looked at all the guys and said, "we have a lot of work to do to prepare for this trip so here's the plan..."

Rhythm Creek Boys
•
R.T.I.
Test Pressing

"The Road Home"

Book Three

Summer 2020

HARRISON HARE'S HISTORY

Everything has a history including the book you just finished reading! The photo below shows the original book which was the last assignment in my high school English class at Adolfo Camarillo High School, (A.C.H.S.),Camarillo California, December 1973. I didn't have any plans to add to it or re-write it until many years later.

Fast forward many years later, 32 years to be exact. I blew the cobwebs off the original and commenced to get serious about doing something with this ancient book I still had. Using the original premise, the story was brought back to life adding new characters and professional illustrations. Self-published in 2017.

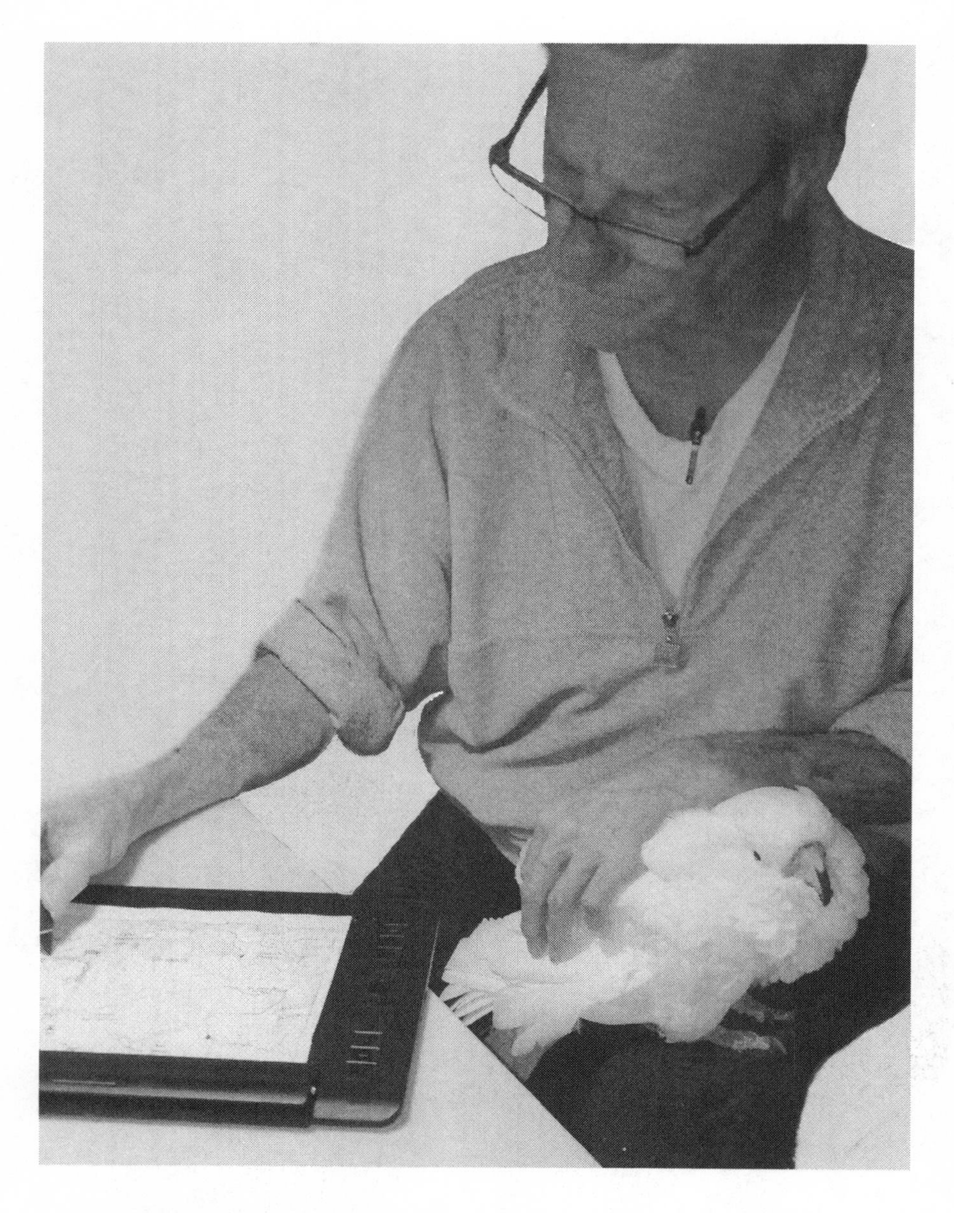

Author Wade Boteler is pictured here working on a drawing making sure Peekaboo, (Bousterama), is not only comfortable but also involved in the process.

Wade resides in So. Cal. with his life partner Kristine, without whom, this work would not exist!

Made in the USA
Lexington, KY
19 September 2019